ALIEN LORD'S CAPTIVE

WARRIORS OF THE LATHAR

MINA CARTER

NEW YORK TIMES & USA TODAY BESTSELLING AUTHOR

WANT THE LATEST NEWS AND CONTESTS?
SIGN UP TO MINA'S NEWSLETTER!
http://mina-carter.com/newsletter/books/

CONTENTS

1

Sergeant Cat Moore walked down the corridor toward the bridge after an all important stop by the coffee machine. To say caffeine was required for the second half of her shift at the traffic control desk would be an understatement.

The graveyard shift was always the worst, and this one was shaping up to be the shift from hell. They'd already had a near-miss in the fighter bay, and two of the bigger troop transports were sporting brand-new paint jobs after both trying to head out on the same flight vector. She didn't even want to think about the fact an Argos-class destroyer had also been assigned the same vector. Forget new paintwork. If that had come in at the same time, they'd have been looking at a new docking arm on the base and a casualty count that made her break out in a cold sweat just at the "what if?"

Sighing, she lifted her mug and sucked down half the blessed java. The sigh of relief escaped her lungs as the hard-hitting stimulant, a compound-caffeine only served in the highly active areas of the base, hit her bloodstream. They did say things came in threes, so surely they were done for tonight?

Wooogahhh-Ahhh-Wooogaaahhh.   Wooogahhh-Ahhh-Wooogaaahhh.

The sound of the sirens filled the corridor, lights flicking from white to red.

"Shit." Red alert. Apparently, they *weren't* done for the night.

Cat threw the half-empty mug at a recycling point, hitting it dead center, and set off down the corridor at a run. She crashed through the double doors to the bridge and emerged into chaos.

"Multiple ships, port side."

"Shields out, sector Four-B!"

"Launch fighters! Sound all-quarters!" That last was the captain yelling orders from the command circle in the center of the bridge. "Send a message to Earth command that we're under attack."

Under attack? Who could possibly be attacking

them? As Cat made her way around the circle to her post, the sound of explosions filled the air, and the deck under her feet lurched, throwing her to the floor. More alarms blared behind her as she scrambled up.

"Massive damage to sectors three, four, and seven. Hull breach in four. Shit...we're being boarded."

"Marshal internal defenses," the captain shouted. "Go into Foothold protocol."

Cat's stomach dropped at the words, as she finally made it to her desk. Her hands shook as she logged into her console. Foothold situation was bad. It meant a superior force was attacking the base and had the numbers to take it. Foothold meant they were in last line of defense mode and all sensitive information needed to be locked down.

She met the quick glance of one of the other traffic control officers. Jessica looked as pale as she felt. They'd all trained for this, but with the only enemy in the area using basic surface to orbit technology, they had never expected to actually use them.

"Who is it?" she mouthed, her hands working on automatic as she cleared all the recent flight logs out of the system. Any ship coming into or leaving the base logged their journey. Since most of them ended up or started from Sentinel Five, that meant any enemy could discover the location of all Terran facilities if they got hold of the records.

"No idea." Jess typed as quickly as she did, clearing records. "They must've been cloaked or something. One minute there was nothing, and then we were surrounded."

"Internal defenses offline in sector four."

"Mass breaches in sectors nine and twelve."

"Foothold defenses in sector four and seven compromised."

"Someone get me marines on the foothold defenses," the captain shouted, his deep voice making both Cat and Jess pause for a moment.

"Too late, Captain. Foothold down. Enemy forces in the central ring."

"Divert all marines to protect primary areas. Get them up here!"

Shiiiit. Whoever they were, they were in the central parts of the orbital base. Cat blinked and renewed her efforts on the logs. She was two-thirds of the way down, her fingers on fire. It would make it so much easier if there was an auto dump on the system, but protocol insisted on manual deletion in case of data loss.

"Shit, data lock," Jess cursed, slamming her fist on the table. She looked up at Cat. "I'm still a quarter live. You?"

"A third." Her screen froze just at that moment, then her deleted records started to reinstate themselves on the screen. Crap. Crap. Crap. That was so not good. "Captain..." she called out in warning. "They're in the system."

"Fuck it!" The bridge paused as Captain Gregson drove his hand into the arm of his chair. "Kallson," he looked at Jess. "Try and lock them out. Moore, get your ass into the mainframe and cut all access but to the command consoles."

"On it." Cat was already moving, clapping Jess on the shoulder as she passed, heading for the back of the bridge.

Adrenalin surging through her system, she yanked open an access panel and climbed through it. There was only one way to access the mainframe, by ladder from the bridge. It was a design feature meant to keep the computer systems protected in the event of an attack. That the computer core was also nestled alongside the main reactor for the entire base, and that someone was firing at the base, was something she preferred not to think about as she started her descent.

Rather than climbing down, she opted for the quick route. Holding the top of the ladder, she clamped the sides with the insides of her heavy combat boots and slid down the first ladder. Her feet hit the mesh plate with a crash, but Cat didn't hang about. Rushing around the semi-circular platform, she grabbed the next ladder to slide down it. Then the next and the next. Four down, six to go.

More explosions rocked the station, one particularly nasty one almost flinging her from the platform and into the shaft below. Heart in her throat, she clung to the railing for dear life. She needed to move faster. Much faster.

"Nearly there," she muttered, her feet hitting the platform. A sign behind the ladder said, "Nine Below Bridge." Decks weren't numbered in the bowels of the station core. They were assigned for their position in relation to the bridge.

Before she could reach the next ladder, there was a crash and boom above her. Instinctively, she looked up to catch the tail end of an explosion. Metal fragments, remnants of bulkheads and ladders tumbled down the shaft, straight toward her.

Her scream was one of fear and self-encouragement as she raced for the ladder. Just one more flight. The skin on her hands burned as she clamped around the ladder and let go. The slide was more of a fall this time as the station lurched under her. She hit the deck and rolled, the tilt of the flooring allowing her to slide into the doorway recess for the computer core.

Her head hit the bulkhead to the side with a sickening crack and she fought to remain conscious. Her heart almost broke her ribs with its frantic pounding; she slapped at the access plate and fell through. Immediately she dived to the side and scrunched into a little ball. The metal crashed into the floor of the shaft as the doors slid shut, the narrow gap spewing a deadly spray of shrapnel.

The barrier closed, and she was on her feet. Running across the floor was like trying to run on a carnival cakewalk. She slipped as the base rocked with more explosions, fervent prayers falling from her lips that one of those shots wouldn't hit the reactor core above her head. At least if it did, she wouldn't feel a thing. Death would be quick. Instantaneous. No suffering.

She grabbed onto the computer core console. For such an impressive system, the main control panel was surprisingly simple. Just three monitors and input panels.

Something hit the other side of the door, hard.

It sounded like claws screamed against the metal—fingernails down a chalkboard. Her blood chilled, but she kept typing, even when the door behind her cracked open with a squeal. She drilled down, reaching the star charts and any other information regarding Terra-central system. Metal clicked on metal behind her and her legs began to shake.

What was back there? She couldn't look...not yet. A small moan whispered from her lips as, at any moment, she expected a laser bolt in the back. Records collated, she dumped the data, clearing the system finally.

Data-dump complete. No records found.

She almost collapsed on the console with relief. Whatever happened to Sentinel Five, these assholes wouldn't find their way to earth.

The noises behind her stopped. There was no breathing though. Odd.

Slowly, Cat turned.

And looked into the face of a monster.

A red "eye" in a smooth, flat face studied her. Manlike, it stood on two legs, but there the resemblance ended. It lifted its hand, complete with razor sharp claws and she screamed, the sound of her own terror the last thing she heard as she tumbled into darkness.

"Well?" War Commander Tarrick K'Vaas demanded as his troop leaders surrounded him. The human base had fallen quickly, their defenses no match for Latharian technology. But then, not much was. In their many centuries of roaming the myriad galaxies, the Lathar had never met a species that could match them.

"Little to no resistance," Karryl, one of his senior warriors, complained, his lips compressed into a thin line. "One look at the avatars and half pissed their pants, the rest ran screaming. Did come across some resistance with some of their soldiers. One of the females—can you believe they let women fight? —was rather...determined."

The hint of a smile crossed his lips, and Tarrick shook his head. The big warrior loved to fight, always moaning he could never find an enemy worthy of his skills. The fact that he'd thought enough of the human woman to mention her meant she was probably a one-woman army.

"Gaarn? Jassyn? Talat?" He turned to his other commanders, ignoring the mass of humans the avatars were crowding into the defeated base's flight deck. Some were bloody and bruised, others even unconscious, he noted as an avatar laid a woman in the same gray uniform as the rest on the deck. He frowned at the blood on one side of her face. If some fool avie-pilot had injured one of the women without reason, he would be pissed. Without women of their own, the Lathar prized all females, even... Tarrick shuddered, the Oonat.

Unfortunately, the Oonat, with their flat faces and multiple breasts, were one of the few species genetically compatible with the Lathar. He'd never taken one to his bed, but without offspring, he knew that day was soon coming. It would be a one-time stand, though, not even a night. Oonat tended to fall pregnant immediately. With multiple births, he would have the sons he needed to continue the Vaas line and he needn't bed such a creature again.

He paused for a moment to consider the unconscious woman. Even unaware, she had curves that caught his interest and triggered something in his male psyche. He couldn't see her face, but a quick scan of the other females revealed pleasing features, not unlike the Lathar. In fact, apart from their smaller physical size, even the men, they could *be* Lathar. Almost. Their eyes were different. Not the myriad colors of his people's.

"How about the rest of you?" he shot the question at the other senior warriors.

"Same, Commander." Jassen was the first to reply. Quietly spoken, he didn't often speak , but when he did, others listened. "Little to no capable resistance, but a lot of courage. Technological they are eons behind us. The avies seem to terrify them."

Tarrick saw that for himself, watching as the remotely piloted avatar robots moved between the humans. They cowered, scrambling to get away from the machines or curling up on themselves when they couldn't.

"Have you found her?" he demanded, reminding them of their secondary reason for being here.

The first was because the station had women, and the Lathar needed women. The second was because of one woman in particular. The one that had sealed the fate of the rest on this little alien base. All his senior warriors had been present when they'd listened to recorded transmissions from this place and he'd heard it. A female's voice, soft and melodious. Nothing special, but it struck a chord deep inside him, flipped a switch and changed him. Since that day, he'd been stronger, faster, more capable as a warrior.

"The avies are looking for her," Karryl answered. "Trying to match a voice print, but nothing so far."

"Keep looking," he ordered, planting his feet in a wide stance and folding his arms. "I want her found..."

For some reason, his gaze wandered to the unconscious woman again. Would this little creature with her mouth-watering curves be the woman with the bewitching voice? If she were, he would even be content with having to bed an Oonat to bear his sons. Given the Lathar's twisted history and genetics that had seen all their women die out and breeding with other species almost impossible, there was no way they'd be lucky enough for humanity to be compatible. But he could keep a more pleasing countenance in his mind as he rutted, he could present her with his child to raise as their own.

A smile curved his lips as he walked across the flight deck. A woman at his side and sons to carry on his name, what more could a warrior ask for?

2

"Cat! *Cat!* Oh, god, Cat, wake up."

Cat came to, slowly becoming aware someone was rocking her shoulder. Opening her eyes, she slammed them shut as agony sliced through her brain.

"Ugh..."

Carefully, she tried again to find Jessica sat over her, concern written on her features. A livid bruise covered one side of her face and her eyes were haunted.

"What happened?" Cat whispered, her voice barely more than a sliver of sound between them. Struggling to sit up, she nodded her thanks when Jess slid an arm around her. Hell, that blow to the head in the core had really knocked her about.

Memory returned...the metal monster and she gasped. "There are—"

"Shhh," Jess whispered, her eyes wide and fixed on something beyond Cat. "They don't like us talking."

"They?"

Thunk-whir-thunk-whir-thunk.

The sound penetrated Cat's consciousness a second before the red-eyed monster from her memory shoved its face into hers. She stifled a scream, scrambling backward and knocking Jess out from its reach, but it followed her. Dropping to all fours, its metal claws scraped on the deck before, like lightning, its "hand" wrapped around her ankle in a punishing grip. This time her scream was real. It dragged her beneath it, her kicks and punches on its metal shoulders and ribcage doing nothing but bruising her. The other hand shot out to wrap around her throat. The tip of the razor sharp talons scraped the back of her neck and her body went weak with fear.

"*Ohgodohgodohgod,*" she whimpered, trying to get her own fingers between the metal of its fingers and her throat. If it wanted to throttle her though, she was a goner.

Its eye focused on her, moving over her face as

though searching for something. Finally, it spoke, haltingly, as though unsure of the language. "Talk. More...words. Talk more words."

Words? She'd give it words.

"Get your fucking freaky metal ass *off* me!" she yelled, and on instinct drove her knee up into its groin area. Her words were echoed by a yelp of pain as her knee reminded her that flesh and bone didn't come off well in a battle against steel...or whatever these creatures were made of.

It swiveled its head on its neck to look down at her knee. "You damage yourself. Why?"

She lost it, screaming back, trying to pry the fingers from around her throat. It was playing with her, taunting her before it killed her. Fuck. That. She wasn't going down without a fight. Granted, resistance against a creature like this might be akin to an ant arguing with a boot, but she sure as hell was going to try.

The sound of whirring and clicking told her more of the creatures had arrived and she screamed something unintelligible at Jess to run. The clicking was joined by the sound of heavy boots on the deck plates.

A deep voice growled something that her ears couldn't make sense of and instantly, the metal creature let go of her. Gasping, she scrambled backward, ignoring the complaint of her injured knee in favor of putting distance between her and it.

Her hand met Jess's boot and without looking away from the metal creature, she all but climbed up the leg, trying to push them both away. When Jess wouldn't move, she realized her hands rubbed against a distinctly non-female body. A strong arm wrapped around her waist, holding her securely when her legs shook and wouldn't hold her. The silence around them finally penetrated her brain and she turned her head slowly to meet the eyes of the man who held her.

"Hmm...hi?"

He wasn't human. Although, why the hell she thought he was with creatures like the metal monster running around, she had no idea. He looked human though. But like an upgraded, better version of human or something. Taller than any man she'd ever seen, his shoulders were broad and muscled, and the rest of him that she'd practically plastered herself to was equally as hard and muscled. Hell, even his muscles had muscles. And that pressure against her stomach...oh shit. She blinked. That couldn't be his cock. No way...no guy had a cock that...that...

He wasn't human.

For all she knew he could have two cocks. Her head began to swim... his face wavering in and out of focus. What was wrong with her?

He smiled, tiny lines appearing around his eyes and reached up with his free hand to touch her cheek.

"Ve'lani," he murmured and bent his head to claim her lips.

Which was when her head decided that enough consciousness was enough and dropped her back into the darkness.

IT WAS HER. The deliciously curved, little human female was the one they were looking for.

As soon as the signal came through from one of Karryl's avie-pilots that he'd found a voice match, Tarrick had set off at a run across the flight deck. The human women scattered this way and that, but he ignored them. Now the property of the Lathar, they needed to get used to warriors running about, since most would end up claimed by one eventually.

He reached the avatar-bot, and a surge of anger filled him that the pilot had the little female pinned down by her throat. That didn't stop her fighting back though. Amusement filled him for a second as she screamed right in the face of the avatar. She had no way of knowing, but that kind of high-pitched sound would overload the bot's auditory sensors and give the pilot an earful of static.

"Let her go, *now*," he ordered and the pilot released his grip. Instantly, the woman bolted from beneath it. The bots weren't sexual in any way, shape, or form, but he still didn't like the sight of her pinned beneath it like that. She scuttled across the floor on her ass toward him, hand brushing his boot. Within a heartbeat, she clambered up him, her small, trembling body pressed against his as she used him for balance.

His protective instincts surged to the fore and he wrapped an arm around her waist. He hadn't realized when she was lying down but standing and pressed against him, he became aware of just how small she really was. Child-like tiny, but the body under his hands was all woman. All. Woman.

His cock surged to life at the touch of her small hands, even as the violent trembles that raked her body triggered his primal male need to protect. She was fixated on the avie-bot, still crouched a few steps from them, the pilot no doubt in a panic that he'd angered Tarrick. His men both respected and feared him in equal measure. He was fair, to a point, but a man's claimed woman was an entirely different matter and to lay hands on one without permission...

She looked up at him and all such matters were instantly wiped from his mind. Dark curls surrounded her small, heart-shaped face, falling around her shoulders in glorious disarray. Dark brown, with hints of red and black, it was a color he'd never seen before. Lathar hair was one color, no tones, didn't shimmer and entice the touch of his hands like hers. But her hair paled in comparison to her eyes, a warm color that reminded him of the forests near his home. Of the soft leaves of the Herris blossom tree at the bottom of his father's garden and the smile of his mother, a fading but cherished memory now.

Blood still covered her temple and cheek, which worried him, but he couldn't resist reaching out to touch her soft skin, smiling to ease the fear he saw in her eyes.

"Beautiful," he whispered, wishing he knew enough of her language to reassure her everything would be okay now. That she was safe in his arms... in his bed.

Touch led to other needs and the urge to claim her lips overwhelmed him. A willing slave to the impulse, he leaned down and brushed her lips with his. They were soft and warm, and her soft intake of breath urged him on.

A groan welled up in his chest as her lips became pliant. She welcomed his touch...immediately submissive. Triumph swelled within him and he tugged her closer to deepen the kiss. Then her head fell back, her body heavy in his arms.

She'd slipped back into unconsciousness.

"Fuck," he hissed, gathering her limp form into his arms. "If you've damaged her in any way," he growled at the crouching avatar, knowing the pilot could hear him. "Then you'd better start praying to the gods. Hear me?"

The bot tucked its head, movement relayed from its pilot to avoid looking Tarrick in the face. He strode past it, toward the flyers he and his warriors used to board the base. "Alert Healer Laarn that his services are required, and start loading the women. Leave the men, they're worthless."

His warriors scrambled to do his bidding, and Tarrick ducked his head to step into the flyer, his precious bundle in his arms.

"Back to the *Velu'vias*," he ordered the pilot and

settled himself into one of the jump seats behind the cockpit. He didn't bother strapping in, not for the short journey back to the destroyer. Not like anyone was going to attack with the might of a Lathrian war group surrounding the base.

He looked at the woman in his arms. She lay curled in his lap. A perfect fit, as though she belonged there, and again, he marveled at how small she was. How perfectly formed. Dark eyelashes fluttered against her cheeks and he could see the steady beat of the pulse in her throat. His panic over her collapse receded a little. Stress perhaps? Latharian women, when still in existence, had been delicate creatures. Highly strung, they'd been susceptible to stress, which explained the highly protective instincts of the male warriors. His little female need not worry about anything ever again, he vowed, holding her carefully. She was his and he would do anything to protect such a precious gift from the Goddesses.

The journey to his flagship, the *Velu'viass*, was brief. The pilot had no sooner engaged the engines before he was throttling back to bring the transporter to a soft landing in the main flight bay. Tarrick gathered the woman securely into his arms and stood, nodding to the pilot as he exited the craft.

He didn't voice his approval of the smooth ride or otherwise indicate his mood. It would be neither expected nor looked for. Their culture was hard and if his warriors didn't perform as expected, he'd replace them.

His boots rang out on the deck as he headed through the corridors toward the healing bay. No one mentioned the fact he carried the human woman in his arms, and any curiosity was carefully kept under wraps. As a K'Vass and the commander to boot, his actions were beyond question.

Apart from for one person anyway...

He strode through the doors to the healing bay and laid the human on the nearest diagnostic unit before lifting his head to yell. "Laarn! Get your lazy ass out here!"

Like the rest of the ship, the healing bay was devoid of luxuries and decoration. Each bed unit was set in an alcove created by the internal bulkheads and support structures. Summoned by his shout, a tall figure stepped around the corner at the end of the bay. Broad shouldered with the build of a warrior, he wore a warrior's leathers like Tarrick, but with the teal sash of a healer instead of red for command. Except for the long hair and the fact his eyes were green instead of gold, Tarrick might as well have been looking in a mirror.

"Lazy?" His twin raised an eyebrow as he strolled closer. "Do you have any idea of the delicate experiments your bellow just destroyed?"

"Will you ever learn to respect your Lord, healer?" Tarrick demanded, but his lip was already beginning to quirk up into a smile.

"When you learn to respect your elders, pup," Laarn snorted his standard response. Born a few minutes before Tarrick, he often reminded his brother of the fact. Even as he spoke though, Laarn's attention wasn't on Tarrick, but on the still form of the woman on the bed. "What have you brought me this time? You really should resist picking up every waif and stray you find, you know."

"Asshole healer."

"Dickhead warrior."

The affectionate banter trailed off as Laarn stepped forward to the side of the unit. Recognizing the presence of the healer, the diagnostic bed flared to life. A holofield covered the form on the bed in an arc of shimmering blue. Symbols that meant nothing to Tarrick crawled over its translucent surface.

"This is one of the humans?" Laarn asked as a

diagram of the woman's skeleton formed on the display. Leaning forward, Laarn tucked a long strand of hair behind his ear as he examined the skull area. Tarrick leaned in and breathed a sigh of relief when there was no apparent damage.

"Yes."

"And you're sure it's fully grown?" Laarn's fingers moved on the input panel and the machine scanned her bodily systems.

"Have you actually *looked* at her? Instead of those dry readouts?" Tarrick raised his eyebrow. "Any idiot can see she's an adult."

Laarn snorted. It was his default expression around his brother. "Yeah. Well, not every species expresses maturity in the same way. For all we know, what we consider a physically mature appearance might be a juvenile for her species."

No. There was no way she could be a juvenile. The fates couldn't be so cruel as to present him with a female who finally interested him, tugged at his soul, for her to be a child.

"No...they all looked like this. And some of them were warriors as well, so unless their species sends its children to war, she has to be an adult."

"Hmmm...Yeah, I think you're right." Laarn intently studied a list scrolling over the display. "All the hormones and neurotransmitters are very similar to ours, and would suggest she is mature."

Snapping off the holo display, Laarn moved around her, running strong hands down her limbs to check for breaks. Tarrick had seen him do this often with other patients. Even though he used the diagnostic beds a lot, Laarn never trusted them, saying they weren't as sensitive as a healer's hands.

Tarrick gritted his teeth as the urge to knock his twin aside and snatch the woman out of his grasp assailed him. He trusted Laarn more than he did the rest of his sworn warriors, so his jealousy was out of character.

"And what were you doing when she passed out?"

"Err," Tarrick paused for a moment. "Kissing her."

Laarn stopped his examination to look up. "So... her base has been attacked by technologically advanced beings, she's sustained injuries in said attack, then is captured by an avatar-bot...which, in case you failed to realize is probably the stuff of nightmares for her. Then you, an alien, kisses her..." He blew out a breath, blowing the bangs out of his face. "Goddesses, give me strength, were you born an idiot, or are you making a special effort today?"

The machine beeped before Tarrick could reply, and Laarn's brows snapped together when he read the message on the display. "That's odd."

"What is?" Tarrick crowded forward." Is she okay?"

She had to be okay. He needed her to talk to him, needed to try to figure out why her voice called to him so much.

"Get your fat ass out of the cleaner field. You don't know where she's been and I'm not letting her loose until she's clean down to her skin." Laarn waved him back irritably as he studied the machines readouts, and then grunted. "Nope. The machine is wrong. I'll run it through maintenance routines later."

Stepping to the side, he prepped two medi-patches before pushing up one of her sleeves and pressing them to her skin. Almost instantly, the patches turned translucent and dissolved beneath the surface.

"Standard biotic in case she's brought anything aboard or reacts badly to anything onboard. I've also added a shot of ker'ann; I assume you intend to bed her. She's so small, she'll need a little help if you expect her to take you," Laarn said, his light eyes unreadable. "The   second   contains   a   neuro-translator. It'll make its way to the correct area in her cortex and install our common languages. From the scans, we shouldn't have any problems with linguistic compatibility."

"Excellent. My thanks." Tarrick stepped forward, unable to wait to get her into his arms again.

"You're welcome. Are... are there more like her?"

Tarrick stopped, his little human in his arms and halfway off the bed, to look at his twin. "There are. Why?"

Although they were near identical, and Laarn was easily as deadly a warrior as Tarrick himself, he'd never once expressed an interest in females. Oh, he had all the male drives, but Tarrick got the feeling it had always been a physical function for Laarn, rather than a pleasure.

Laarn shrugged, picking at an invisible speck of lint on his sash. "They're different. New. Interesting. I might want one for study."

"*Just* for study?" Tarrick grinned, holding his woman closer. "And there are, but you might want to get down to the holding cells quickly. More than one warrior has his eye on claiming a human."

3

*C*at hadn't had many concussions in her life, but she knew what they felt like. This, when she awoke on a large, soft bed to see a steel beamed roof above her, was *not* how they felt. The fuzziness and weird feeling was there, but everything else, the pain and nausea, was absent.

That blessing paled into insignificance though as she realized she was being watched.

In a chair opposite sat the largest man she'd ever seen. With a gasp she pushed upright and scuttled backward until she hit the headboard. He studied her, an unreadable expression on his face. Hand shaking, she shoved her hair out of her face.

"Who are you? Where am I?"

Keeping him in her line of sight, she risked a quick look around. They were alone in what looked like a bedroom. Memory filtered back and her blood ran cold. The attack on the base, the metal monsters —robots she now realized—and...the alien who had kissed her.

Him.

"Tarrick."

"Say what?" She blinked in surprise, attention all on him again. He hadn't moved, but only an idiot would think he wasn't a threat. Danger clung to him like a second skin, inherent in every line of the big, muscled body. With those golden, slitted eyes, so odd in what looked like a very human face, he reminded her of a big cat.

Would he eat her all up? Heat hit her cheeks, her body humming as she pushed the thought away. He wasn't human, so who was to say his idea of sex would be the same as hers? For all she knew, she could be the appetizer for his main meal or something.

"Tarrick," he growled the word again, but before she could ask, he spoke again. "It's my name. Yours?"

Name. He wanted her name. She allowed herself a small sigh of relief. Okay, that boded well. Most people didn't introduce themselves to their meals. With the introduction, she realized he spoke perfect English. Fuck, she was so screwed.

"Moore, Cat. Sergeant. Three-seven-five-alpha-four-seven-nine," she replied automatically. She'd slipped up by asking him questions, Terran fleet protocol was to give out only the mandated information.

He shifted, gaze still on her. Was that a hint of a smile she saw on his lips before he covered them with his hand?

"Your people use numbers as names, Moore Cat?"

She treated him to the "Moore look," a gift from her grandmother, and lifted a hand to check her temple. She'd fallen, she remembered the feeling of blood running down her cheek. But there was nothing. She looked at her fingers in confusion. Okay...

"My healer sorted your injuries, little Moore Cat. Does it still hurt?"

His voice was closer. She looked up and stifled a gasp to see him leaning forward, arms rested on his knees. The leather top he wore pulled against the heavy muscle of his shoulders and arms, but it was his look that was more intimating. Utter focus. On her. It was like being viewed under a microscope. Unsettling.

"Moore, Cat. Sergeant. Three-seven-five-alpha-four-seven-nine," she repeated, stubbornly. Alien dude might be the hottest thing she'd ever seen, even with those weird eyes and all muscled, but that didn't mean he was getting any information out of her.

"Really? You think I don't know a standard response when I hear it?" His lips quirked again and he sat back. Amusement danced in his expression. "Little human, I'm not trying to get information out of you. I'll have all the information I want once my AI reconstructs your computer core."

"Reconstruct?" She allowed herself a small smile. "Hard to reconstruct from data that's no longer there."

"No longer there?" He rubbed strong fingers against what looked like an equally strong jaw with just a bit of a five o'clock shadow. "Now why would that be a problem? Your computer is ridiculously simple, it won't take the AI long to reconstruct the deleted data from the traces in the system."

Her blood ran cold. If they could get that data

back...they could find the other bases, even find Earth.

"You can't...it's deleted," she whispered. "I deleted it myself. Directly in the computer core."

"You? A female?" He blinked, apparently surprised, then smiled. "Do you take me for a fool? No commander would trust a female with such an important task, women are too delicate."

So sexy alien was a chauvinistic asshole. He lost some sex appeal for that. She gave him the look again for good measure.

"Does it still hurt?" He nodded toward her head, a look of concern on his face.

Debating for a moment, she gave a little shake. What could it matter if she admitted that? Not like it was giving away any secrets. "No. Your healer is excellent at his job. Normally I'd have a headache after a knock like that."

Anger tightened his features for a moment, and she was reminded even though this chat was pleasant, he was an alien. Of a species she'd never seen before. Oh, she'd seen the more primitive species the fleet had discovered in its travels, but humanity had gotten used to being the top dog in the area.

Until today.

"I regret that you suffered an injury," he said tightly.

She drew back, wariness running down her spine. With the danger that emanated from him, she didn't want to risk his anger turning toward her.

Crap, was there a way out of here? Trying to make it look like she wasn't looking, she studied the room. Doors to the left, but they were narrow and set into the walls, more like closet doors, and a larger door, big enough for even his shoulders to fit through, on the right.

"Rest assured, the pilot who caused such pain will be disciplined," he closed his eyes, lifting a hand to run through the close-cropped hair. It was all she needed. Heart pounding in her chest, she leaped off the bed and made a break for the door. A stifled yelp broke from her as she skidded and collided with the doorframe, but her flight was spurred on by the shout and sounds of pursuit behind her.

The door led to another room with a desk and bigger doors on the other side. A cry already forming in the back of her throat, she hit them running and fell into the corridor beyond. Right into the path of two of the robots.

"Shit...no!" She twisted to the side, trying to wriggle between them before they could stop her, but they were too quick and blocked her path. Rising to her feet, she backed slowly, in case a quick movement would make them attack.

Her back hit something warm and solid. She froze, closing her eyes.

"On a scale of one to ten, how dead am I?"

TARRICK WASN'T EASILY SURPRISED, but his little human had managed it. He'd barely closed his eyes before she sprinted from the room with an unexpected turn of speed. Bellowing a warning to the bots on guard, he followed her, but she was fast —damn fast—through the doors to his office before he was halfway across the room.

He followed to find her stepping away from the bots. Neither had touched her, their metallic arms spread wide to stop her escape as he'd ordered. She hadn't curled up in a little ball of terror though, as many who weren't used to the bots did, but instead was backing up slowly.

Into him.

"Dead?" Her words didn't make sense. "Why would I harm a female?"

"Huh? You don't hurt women?" She turned, a look of surprise on her delicate features. Impatient, he waved the bots back to their posts. Now she knew she couldn't get away, he doubted she'd try to run again. She was intelligent, unlike other species he'd come across. The Oonat were passive, but not his little human.

He'd seen the flash of anger and other emotions in her eyes as she'd stubbornly refused to answer him. Oh, undoubtedly her intelligence levels would be well below his, but there was a chance he might have a decent conversation with her. That possibility interested him, and if he was honest, was more than a little arousing.

"No, little Moore Cat." His voice deepened, her presence bringing out the rougher edge, as he reached up to slide his hand into her hair. She flinched, and tried to step away to put distance between them, but he had her. His hand cupped the back of her neck and he held her still. "Calm yourself. I won't harm you."

"Really..." She held herself rigid, subtle resistance to his touch. He whispered his thumb over her cheek. Laarn had healed her, so she wouldn't faint if he kissed her again.

"Try it, alien, and I'll bite your face off," she hissed, snapping her teeth together.

He couldn't help the soft chuckle that escaped him, a sound of amusement he couldn't remember ever having made before. Bending his head, he touched his lips to hers. The slide of skin over skin caught him in its seductive coils, teasing his senses. Unable to stop, he tugged her closer.

She put her hands on his chest, trying to push, but it wouldn't work. She was his, by right of conquest. He angled his head and demanded access with a sweep of his tongue.

She held still for a moment, frozen against him. Then her fingers curled into claws, clutching for purchase on his leathers as a delicate shiver raced through her. So his little human wasn't immune to him. Pulling her flush against him, he used his free hand to press her hips to his. His cock, fully engorged, pressed against her softer form and she gasped. He took the opening and deepened the kiss.

Her taste exploded on his tongue, and he groaned, resisting the urge to crush her to him and explore more fully. She tasted of Jenin berries and starla water, tastes of the exotic but so familiar he couldn't remember them ever not being part of his life.

Her tongue touched his, tentatively, and he paused. Waited. Was it a mistake, or had she meant that? The shy touch came again. He growled, letting the male animal free a little and kissed her again. Deeper. Hotter. Twining his tongue around hers, he stroked and teased, letting her see his passion. A glimpse of what she could expect in his bed.

But this was not the time, or the place. Breaking away, he allowed himself a final taste of her lips before looking down. Her eyes were wide and dark, hazy with desire. Just the sight made his cock pulse savagely.

"Don't look at me like that, Moore Cat, or we'll finish this here and now."

HE'D KISSED her like there was no tomorrow.

"Finish? Over my dead body." Breathing heavily, Cat pushed away and added a glare for good measure. Where had that come from? It was like as soon as he touched her, all common sense left the building.

He folded his arms, looking all intimidating and growly. "You will not refuse me, little Moore Cat."

"Cat. It's Cat," she corrected him. Anything to get him off the subject of where ever *that* had been heading. Stepping back, she nearly collided with one of the robots. With a squeak she jumped forward again. "What the hell *are* those things?"

"The bots? They're avatars."

Reminded of their presence, she drew closer to him. The danger he posed was infinitely different to the robots. At least with him, she wasn't worried he'd rip her limb from limb.

"Like a physical representation of something?"

He nodded, a look of surprise on his face. "Exactly. They're operated via a neural link by specialist pilots."

So they weren't mindless killing machines. She turned to study them with interest. That made sense. The one that had pinned her on the flight deck seemed unsure of the language.

"Pilots like you?" She slid him a sideways glance. That he was military was undeniable, she recognized the manner and bearing. "The same species as you, whatever you are."

"We are the Lathar." His voice rang with pride and he extended a hand to indicate she should precede him. She stepped forward quickly, moving past the creepy robots. Down the corridor was not back into the bedroom, which was good... Okay, she had to argue with her ovaries on that one, since all her feminine instincts were clamoring for her to climb tall, alien, and handsome like a frigging tree.

"And no, not exactly like me," he continued, falling into step beside her. Automatically he measured his steps by her shorter stride, a consideration she hadn't expected. "Pilots are warrior level. I am War Commander. In charge of this ship."

She arched her eyebrow, detecting the note of command in his voice. "Then you are not a warrior?"

He shot her a look, ignoring the two leather-clad men who passed them. They wore sashes as well, but in a different color to Tarrick's. "Not just a warrior, no."

"Huh." She fell into silence, wondering where he was taking her. So far, this alien attack wasn't at all what she expected. Her questions were soon answered when they reached the end of the corridor and a set of double doors opened in front of her. She stifled a gasp and spun behind Tarrick.

The room was filled with warriors, all with different colored sashes. Most were congregated on one side of the room, opposite floor to ceiling windows that looked out onto something she couldn't see from this angle.

A smaller group of men stood near the glass, and as the door opened, one of them turned. His face split into a smile.

"Tarrick! Come join us, we're studying the humans, deciding which ones we want."

THE CHILL EMANATING from his little human's expression warned Tarrick that Karryl's comment was not popular. He watched her in his peripheral vision as they approached the group of senior warriors. Her back was stiff, like she had a support strut for a spine, and her expression so blank and forbidding that if he hadn't seen emotions playing over her face earlier, he'd have suspected humans didn't have them.

He knew the instant she spotted the human women in the holding cells below. With a gasp, she rushed to the window. Below were ten cages, for want of a better word, each containing at least twenty women from the base. Just the youngest and fittest. The older women would be shipped off and sold as servants throughout the Latharian empire.

"Oh my god, what are you doing to them?" she demanded, her small hands on the glass as she watched a couple of avatars stalk between the cages. The women in the cells shrank back as the bots passed, fear on their faces.

She whipped around, pinning him with an overbright glare. "Let them out. Now!"

Karryl grunted in surprise but didn't say anything. The rest of the room was likewise silent, a fact she became aware of slowly. She looked around, her gaze darting to some of the warriors before returning to him, and her skin paled.

"Until they have been claimed, they will remain in the cells." His voice was quiet but firm, carrying easily.

"Claimed?" She frowned but didn't relinquish her position by the glass. Her concern for the women below was evident. "What do you mean 'claimed'?"

She knew what he meant, he knew she did. It showed in the looks she shot the warriors around him, incensed and protective at the same time. It showed in the way she backed against the window, as though putting herself between the Latharian warriors and the women below.

"You're not stupid, Moore Cat. Each woman below will end up in one of my warrior's beds. Why else do you think we took your base?" He folded his arms over his chest. "You have nothing else we need. Your technology is primitive, I'm surprised you even got out of your own system, and your military capability is laughable. We didn't even need half our combat-bots to break your base wide open."

She shook her head, but he carried on anyway. "Your women, little human. That's what we were after. A prize more precious than jewels or rare minerals and ores."

He stalked toward her, not paying attention to the other warriors in the room. This was between them. She backed, pressed against the glass, but he didn't stop until he could feel the heat of her skin against his. Tucking his fingers under her chin, he made her look up.

"You are ours, you all belong to the Lathar. The quicker you accept that, the happier your lives will be."

Her skin was still pale, but her eyelids fluttered down as she dropped her gaze. Approval rolled through him. She knew her place already. This was good, perhaps these humans would integrate quickly and well into Latharian society. Such a boon he hadn't expected. Most new species had to be broken and retrained.

"Women are prized in our culture. All of you will be well treated."

"Yeah, as long as we fuck on command, right?"

She lifted her head and enmity glittered in her hard gaze. He had less than half a second's warning before her hand shot out. She slapped him across the cheek, the sharp crack of skin on skin ringing through the room. A gasp followed, several warriors taking a step forward, hands on their weaponry.

He held his hand up to stop them, struggling to contain his anger. No one laid a hand on the War Commander, not if they valued their lives.

"I've been patient with you so far, Cat." Leaning forward, he invaded her personal space, voice low and dangerous. "But do not push me. Believe me, you and your women are in a far better position than if another species had found you first. The Krin, for example, view the flesh of other races as somewhat of a delicacy."

He reached out to run a finger down her arm where the fabric of her uniform was torn away. "I can only imagine what they would make of such soft skin. They'd hunt your kind into extinction."

She shivered, biting her lip, her skin even paler than it was before. He knew he was scaring her, but he had no reason to conceal the facts. The truth of the matter was that her kind would be safer with the Lathar as their masters. At least then they would survive as a species rather than become a fading memory on an interstellar menu.

Looking up, she met his gaze. "So we prostitute ourselves for protection, is that it?"

Something in her dark gaze struck at his heart, an organ he'd thought shriveled and empty long ago, and he reached out to stroke a thumb over her cheekbone.

"It doesn't have to be that way. Your women will get a choice in the claiming, on one condition."

She frowned, her expression wary. "Define choice, and what condition?"

Tarrick bit back his smile. His little human was shrewd, but he had her right where he wanted her. Her concern for her fellow humans was the web he'd use to trap her.

"By choice, I mean they can accept or refuse a warrior's claim." That much was already written into law, not that she'd know that. "Up to three times. If they refuse a third time, they will be sold to the pleasure houses to prove comfort for many. I would advise any woman against that. If they have the choice, being a warrior's woman is far preferable." From the shudder that ran through her, she appeared to agree.

"And the condition...you, my little Moore Cat, do not get that luxury." He held her gaze, sliding his hand into the hair at the nape of her neck. Bending his head, he whispered his lips over hers. "You are mine."

4

*C*at had never been so scared or aroused in her life. The silence from the other warriors around them told her there was no help from that quarter, and inches of thick glass separated her from the women in the hold.

She was alone, utterly alone, and helpless.

She lifted her chin and met his gaze. No, not helpless. Never that. She was a Moore through and through and her parents hadn't raised a quitter. So what if her current situation sucked donkey balls? She did have one—no two—advantages.

One, according to Tarrick, his species prized women. Two, he wanted her enough to make her acceptance of him mandatory. Rather than be pissed that he'd taken away what little choice she had left, she found it flattering. Kind of. He was big, sexy, and obviously the boss. She could work with that.

"I have your word that none of my women will be harmed?" She kept her voice quiet, between them. Even though she kept a straight face, heat at his closeness surged through her veins and pooled between her legs.

His gaze shifted, searching hers, but then he nodded. "You have my word."

She sighed, closing her eyes, and her next words sealed her fate. "I accept your condition."

He didn't speak. Instead, he captured her wrist in one large hand and pulled. They left the large room, the warriors parting before them like water on the prow of a boat. She didn't look at any of them, heat rising in her cheeks. After that little altercation, there was no question of what was happening. Where they were going.

Sure enough, within a minute she could see the doors to his quarters, still with the robotic guards in place. He pulled her past them without a word, bundling her through the outer room and into the bedroom. His sharp bark at the door closed it behind them, an extra click telling her it was locked.

She tried to pry her wrist loose, but it was no good. His grip was like iron. Her breath coming in short pants, she looked up at him to find his cat-like eyes fixed on her. The irises were wider, more rounded now, like human eyes. Desire and need shimmered in their depths.

"You have beautiful eyes. Like a cat's." The words were out before she could stop them.

"Really? What is a cat?" he asked softly as he pulled her closer, fitting her against his large, hard body. He was big, all over. Even... She swallowed, nervousness filling her at the feel of his huge cock pressed close and personal against her belly.

"I-it's a small animal on earth," she managed, her voice stuttering as his hand slid around her waist again. Strong fingers began to pull her uniform shirt from her pants. Hurriedly, she reached behind her and clamped her hand down over his. "A pet."

His lips curved, amusement coloring the darkness of his eyes for a moment. "Why? Do I look like a pet to you?"

He bent his head to kiss her, but at the last minute she turned her head. She couldn't make this too easy, despite the fact need hummed through her veins in time with her pulse. Not when he and his kind had kidnaped them all to use as damn sex slaves. Her evasion backfired when his lips found the soft skin of her throat, leaving a trail of white-hot kisses.

"Pet?" She bit back her gasp, her grip on his hand behind her back slipping. "Yeah, you do a little."

"I'll show you pet." He yanked her shirt from the back of her pants and slid his hand beneath. At the same moment, he claimed her lips and the rush of heat that hit her stole any other thought out of her mind.

She moaned, the sound lost under his lips. He pulled her closer, parting her lips to delve within. The touch of his tongue on hers was electric. He kissed her like a starving man suddenly presented with a banquet, determined to gorge himself before the treat was taken away.

All her protests were scattered as the driving need to get closer to him filled her. A gasp breaking from her lips, she pulled at his sash, seeking the fastenings on the jacket beneath with a desperation she'd never felt before. It was all consuming. She had to touch him, more than she needed to breathe.

He moved, helping her by snapping something on the edge of the sash to free it and yanking down the zipper of the jacket. It fastened crosswise, like a biker jacket, and with a sigh of relief she slid her hands within to find no barrier to his skin. He wore nothing beneath the jacket.

His own hands weren't idle. He broke the kiss for a second to yank her uniform shirt free and pull it up over her head. Rather than fight him, she helped, watching his expression as he looked down at her. Awe and reverence tightened his hard, alien features and she could have sworn his golden eyes glowed.

"Perfect," he muttered, taking in the plain cotton bra she wore. It wasn't satin and lace, but it was new, and the pushup design emphasized her cleavage. Reaching out, he snapped the clip between and freed them for his perusal. His thumb whispered over her nipple, which beaded immediately as though begging for his attention. "Just perfect."

She bit her lip as the bra hit the floor, the heat rolling through her becoming harder and more insistent. It felt odd...not like her typical reactions at all. At first she'd put it down to everything being strange, but now she wasn't so sure. She needed him, like really needed him. Needed sex more than she'd ever needed it in her life despite the fact she was a prisoner and he was her alien captor.

He caught her gasp and looked up quickly. His hand closed around the back of her neck and he pulled her closer. "Shhh, it'll be okay, little Cat. It's normal, our healer gave you a ker'ann shot. To make you more...pliable."

Her head shot up, fury trying to fight the arousal running rampant through her body. "You drugged me?"

He walked her backward toward the huge bed, unbuttoning her pants as they went. She whimpered, trying to fight, but it was no good. No sooner had she told herself she couldn't allow this, now that she knew her responses weren't her own, than she found her own hands pushing his jacket from broad shoulders.

"Not really." He kissed along her neck again, his stubble scraping along her shoulder in the most delicious way. What would it feel like between her legs? Her knees weakened at the thought.

"It amplified what was already there. If you didn't already find me attractive, you wouldn't be drawn to me. Wouldn't—" He cut off, sucking in a hard breath as her hand slid between them and cupped him through his pants. "Have my cock in your hand like that."

"Perhaps I plan to rip it off," she panted, wriggling to get closer even as she stroked the thick, hard length of him under the leather. "You really have no idea how we humans mate, do you? For all you know, human females could eat their mates after sex."

"True." He toppled her backward onto the bed, a strong hand at the zipper of her pants. When he couldn't undo the button, he growled and yanked, ripping the fabric in a casual show of strength that took her breath away, and disposing of her pants behind them. Her panties took even less time to remove. "Do they?"

"Ohhhhh..." He slipped a big hand between her thighs, strong fingers parting her pussy lips and finding the slick wetness there. He stroked, collecting the juices of her arousal and used them to circle her clit.

Then he stopped, braced over her and looked down. "Do they, little human?"

"Huh?" She had to blink and refocus on the question. Her hips ached to move, to rock against his hand and claim the stimulation he'd just denied her. "What?"

"Do human females eat their mates after sex?" he asked again, wickedness dancing in his strange eyes.

"Or am I safe to do this?" He rubbed over her clit, sending sparks through her body. Within two strokes though, he stopped, leaving her more frustrated than before.

"No... don't stop," she whimpered, arching her back and trying to rub herself against his fingers. She needed him to touch her. Now. Sooner. Her arousal was alive, tearing at the inside of her veins to be free.

"Am I safe?" he insisted, even though the expression in his eyes said he knew he was in no danger. This was a game of control. One she'd started but knew she'd lose.

"Yes..." Her words ended on a moan. She'd give him whatever answer he wanted. "Just please, touch me."

"You want me to touch you? Like this?" He bent his head to watch as he rubbed her clit. She panted, legs parted wide at his urging, a flush covering her cheeks up to her hairline. What a sight she must present, naked and splayed open wide, her alien captor's hand working between her legs. "Perhaps this as well?"

At that, he slid his hand down to press two fingers against the entrance to her pussy. Slowly, watching her expression, he pushed them inside her. She moaned, biting her lip as he penetrated inch by slow inch. His hands were big, his fingers thicker than a human's, so she felt every inch as he stretched her. Pumped in and out slowly. Once, twice. On the third penetration, he turned his hand, scissoring his fingers within her. The whimper broke free before she could stop it.

"Oh god, yeah. That. More of that."

He gave her more, adding the pad of his thumb over her clit as he worked her body. Drove her arousal higher and higher until she writhed and whimpered in his hold. She couldn't take any more. Needed to...

"Oh, god...I'm coming." She turned her head and buried her face against his shoulder as her orgasm hit. Shattering apart, she came over him as he finger-fucked her, not slowing, but adding pressure against her g-spot that made her eyes cross even as sharp-edged bliss cascaded through her.

"That's it, little Cat, give me your pleasure. Make yourself slick and wet for me," his deep voice murmured in her ear as she rode out the waves.

Then he pulled his hand free to move over her. The sound of leather giving whispered on the air and something hard and hot nudged at the entrance to her cunt. Her eyes snapped open and she looked up to find him watching her.

"Mine." His voice was low and possessive, more a

growl. He pushed forward, bearing down into her. She gasped, eyes widening as his thick cock met the resistance of her body. Shit, he was so big. She'd never take him all. Panic hit her and she started to struggle, but he held her still easily.

"Shhh, it's okay. The ker'ann ...it helps. It makes your body more...supple?" he reassured her and smoothed the hair back from her face. Pushing again, he groaned when her body parted to accept him, his cock sliding into her half an inch.

"Oh god." It felt good. So good she didn't know what she'd been worrying about. On his next push, she arched up to meet him. Then again, and again, until little by little, he'd worked himself all the way inside her.

Hips against hers, he paused, eyes closed and lines of tension etched into his face. Lifting a hand, she stroked his cheek. He shook his head, growling a response. "Hold still, or even the ker'ann won't help you, little human."

Stuff the ker'ann, or whatever it was, she needed him now. Biting her lip, she rocked her hips. Her moan echoed his as sensation shot through her. Hard pleasure spiked, rolling through her body like a dozen automated wrecking bots on a frenzy. Unable to stop herself, she did it again, feeling his cock slide within her, feeding all sorts of interesting sensations to nerve endings she didn't know she had. Sensories no human man, or cock, could ever reach.

"Oh yes, more..."

He growled, grabbing her wrists and hauling them over her head. "If it's more you want, little human, more you'll get."

With that, he drew back, the slide of his cock stroking her inner walls as he withdrew, almost making her come there and then. She wasn't prepared for the thrust back in. Hard and fast, he impaled her and overwhelmed all her drug-enhanced senses in one go. He did it again, pulling back and thrusting until he'd built up a hard and fast rhythm that had her gasping and arching against him. Urging him on with every cell of her body as she strained for release again, reaching the foothills of that peak again faster than she ever had before and racing up to the peak.

"Yes... Oh... Fuck. I'm—"

She shattered again, the pleasure intense and almost blinding. Hard granules of ecstasy, like shards of broken glass burst through her, over her, within her. For every surface they touched, they shattered again and again. A never-ending cycle of pleasure as his cock moved within her.

Through her bliss, she felt him speed up, heard the growl of need as his thrusts got stronger, faster until...He surged within her one last time and stiffened. Throwing back his head, he roared his release as his cock jerked and pulsed within her. Bathed her inner walls with his white-hot seed. Hotter than a human's. She'd never felt when any of her previous lovers had come within her, but she felt his, as though it were another way to remind her that she was his now. Branding her as his property.

He let go of her hands and collapsed over her, not crushing her, but protectively curled around her as their breathing returned to normal. For long moments, she lay there, just listening to him breathe.

"Tarrick?"

He looked up at the sound of his name, golden eyes sated, and his sexy as sin lips curved into a smile. "So, little human, since I'm still alive, I guess this means you don't eat your mates after sex."

"You found me out." She shrugged, walking her fingers over one broad shoulder. "But I have to warn you, we have quite the appetite. You might have bitten off more than you can chew."

He laughed, sliding his hands down to her hips. In a flurry of movement, he turned them both until he was lying on his back and she straddled him. Her groan as he impaled her on his thick cock echoed around the room.

"Really? And I was just getting started as well."

Biting her lip, she closed her eyes and began to ride him.

She'd fucked her very first alien and it wasn't half bad. Okay, scratch that, it was absolutely freaking awesome.

Perhaps being captured by aliens wouldn't work out so badly after all...

5

*T*he alien invasion force had five ships. That wasn't many at all.

Cat Moore stood by a large window in the big room behind the bridge of the alien flagship and studied humanity's opponents. She refused to even think of them as humanity's masters. They might have won a battle by capturing a remote base and enslaving all its personnel, but the war hadn't even started.

Heaven, or whatever gods they worshiped, help them because they thought by sectioning off human women, it would make them docile.

They would learn.

Hand on the cool metal by the window, she glanced over her shoulder. A group of alien warriors clustered around a large table in the middle of the room. They were all big, with more muscles than any man had a right to, and outfitted in leather.

A week ago, she'd have said she'd walked smack bang into the middle of one of her greatest fantasies... ripped, leather-clad aliens were *so* her thing. You'd only have to check her reader to know that. The virtual shelves almost burst with alien romance. But that was all it was. A fantasy. The reality of being claimed by an alien warrior, correction, an alien warrior *lord*, was sexy, but if she had anything to do with it, short-lived.

"So you're saying they should never have left their own system, never mind made it this far?" Tarrick, her captor and would be "Master," asked, his hands resting on the holographic display table in front of him.

She paused for a moment, her attention caught as his muscles pulled at the leather of his uniform jacket. A uniform she knew he wore nothing under. Heat uncoiled to loop through her veins, her intake of breath more a shiver. As a species, the Lathar were big and muscled, but there was that little something extra about Tarrick that hit her on a primitive, female level. If she'd met him in other circumstances, he'd have caught her interest for sure.

Down girl, she reminded herself and folded her arms. *We're making plans to bring about their downfall, not to climb their leader like a tree.*

Infiltration, that's what it was all about. And what better place to do that than from their leader's bed? She flitted a little closer, her steps silent in the delicate sandals she wore.

"I'm surprised they even made it out of orbit," another warrior, Jassyn, replied as he looked over the schematics displayed on the table—records pulled from the Sentinel Five computer that the base commander ordered deleted, but reconstructed by the alien ship's AI. She knew the Sentinel commander issued the order because she'd been the one to wipe them. Right before one of their combat-bots captured her.

Computer wipe was standard operating procedure to ensure all records and star charts remained out of enemy hands. They just hadn't counted on facing a far technologically superior enemy. From what she could work out, the Lathar had ruled the galaxies for generations. One primitive little species like humanity trying to pull a fast one would never work. Not unless they got inventive.

"But somehow, they got out of orbit and seem to have spread like fucking wildfire." Jassyn's hands moved over the console in front of them, flicking documents out of the way to show star charts called from the reconstructed records. Swift movements of his fingers drew lines over the charts and highlighted the edges of what looked like human-held space. She moved closer until she could feel the hum of the holographic field over the table. "They have quite a sophisticated network here. From what I can work out, they also have a subspace communications array with relay points here, here, and here."

*Crap, crap, crap...*how had they figured that out? Far from being the beefcake grunts she'd assumed, Tarrick's warriors were scarily intelligent. *Don't judge a book by its cover.* Her grandmother had been fond of saying that.

Tarrick looked up, his gaze focused on the men around him and not noticing her by the edge of the table. "I thought they just had conventional communications? Subspace is a different matter. Does that mean their central command knows of our presence?"

With any luck, yeah... If command knew about the attack, they'd already have mobilized destroyers to head out to the base. Five ships shouldn't stand a chance against the joint might of the Terran fleet.

"No, I don't believe so." Jassyn shook his head, his long hair dancing on his shoulders. This close she could hear the faint creak of leather when he moved. "Our suppression fields knocked out any outgoing messages as we attacked. Overwhelmed the signal, and before it came back online we had control so nothing's gone out. We've been getting regular pings on the relay since though."

He pushed the star charts to one side and brought up what looked like a communications log. The rest leaned forward to study it, cutting off her view of the table.

"They're assuming technological malfunction? And what's this stuff that looks like dots and dashes?"

"That I don't know yet. It seems to be a layer below the primary communication. Perhaps an echo or some kind of repeater pattern?" Jassyn shrugged, his expression saying he had no clue.

She blinked, hiding her surprise. They hadn't picked up the morse code. She was stunned aliens with such a high level of technology hadn't worked out the simple system. Why hadn't their super-duper computer picked it up? Either way, it was an advantage she'd take, even if she didn't know how to use it at the moment.

"But yes, they seemed to assume malfunction so far," Jassyn continued.

"They haven't encountered an advanced species yet so they weren't expecting us. Without information, they seem to think malfunction rather than attack. But they will want to find out what happened. Given their level of technology, I would expect a ship or two to come and investigate soon. From the records we pulled..." He moved the star chart back to the center of the table. "They have ships here and here. Either of these could make it here within twelve hours."

Twelve hours. She smothered her intake of breath. That wasn't a lot of time for her to find a security lapse to exploit. Not when she was with Tarrick or he had those monster remote piloted robots watching her. She flicked a glance sideways to the door. The metallic arms of the two guards outside were clear to see through the glass. They were always on watch.

"Okay, monitor the communication relays for movement from those ships. I want to know the instant anything changes. Even if they go dark...

Especially if they go dark," Tarrick ordered, flicking a glance at her.

"Moore Cat?" he called out, still mangling her name even though he knew its real format. It seemed to amuse him. *Asshole alien.*

Blanking her expression, she looked at him, her face a porcelain mask. Irritation flashed in his golden cat-like eyes and she suppressed her smirk. He didn't like her poker face. Good.

"You belonged to your species military." He motioned her forward so she took another step, her stomach brushing the edge of the table and looked at the documents laid out. "What should we expect, by way of response?"

Her eyebrow lifted into a delicate arch and it was a moment before she spoke. "Well, it's rather hard to say, to be honest. Our great leaders would have to consult the oracles before plotting a course of action."

"I recall no mention of oracles or prophets." Jassyn's brows snapped together and he rifled through the documents again, looking for further evidence. "In fact, humanity didn't appear to be religious."

"Depends on the situation." She shrugged.

"When in doubt, you can always refer to one of our standard religious signals. I'll show you if you like?"

All eyes in the room turned to her as she lifted a hand, fingers curled into a fist facing away from them. Then she extended her middle finger and smiled.

"And that means 'screw you.' You really think I will help you?"

There were two snorts and Tarrick's expression set. She'd insulted him in front of his senior warriors. That had to bite. No, that had to burn.

The healer standing next to Tarrick snorted with amusement and his face split into a broad grin. "Ha! I like her."

"Humans," Tarrick growled, his hard expression promising retribution. She refused to acknowledge the shiver of need that wormed its way up her spine and smiled back. What would he do if she stuck her tongue out and blew a raspberry at him?

"Tell me about it." The growled complaint came from the big warrior at the end of the table.

His expression hovered somewhere between anger and frustration. "The males were easy to deal with. We worked over a few, showed the others the error of their ways, and they've been quiet as a *gethal* since. The women... *argh!* Half are refusing to eat, at least five keep trying to escape, and all of them refuse to acknowledge any warrior's existence."

The healer nodded, leaning forward. His smile disappeared, replaced by concern. "He's right. I've had to sedate a couple and I'm a little concerned if the fasting continues. None of them will say why they're not eating, so I'm not sure if it's a cultural thing with them. I'm reluctant to let it continue...so perhaps we should force feed them?"

"You do, and they'll make themselves vomit," Cat broke in.

Tarrick looked up, meeting her eyes. "Oh?"

"It's called a hunger strike." She moved away from the table, her movements graceful. Her own clothing was gone when she woke this morning, replaced instead with a thin dress that looked more like a silk nightie. Far from feeling half-naked though, the inner layer of fabric molded to her figure, giving nothing away as the outer layers swirled around her, bunching around her ankles. The effect made her feel like a fairytale princess and she had to resist the urge to twirl just to swish the skirts.

Small pleasures, she reminded herself, don't fall prey to the bigger concerns. Deal with them, don't panic.

"Humans aren't stupid, and we have a pathological allergy to being enslaved. We'd rather starve to death than be slaves. Force feed them and they'll expel whatever you make them eat."

The warriors exchanged startled looks around the table, but it was the big guy who spoke, his lips curled back to display his disgust. "They'd rather die than accept the shelter we offer. How twisted and barbaric is that?"

"It's called free will and choice." She shrugged again. "And you're a fine lot to talk about barbarism. Not a benevolent superior race, are you? Rather than helping a less able race to defend itself. Rather than guide and aid...you storm in and enslave. Humans, for all our primitive and barbaric ways, outlawed slavery centuries ago."

The warrior snorted and she rounded on him, anger surging through her. "What if it were the other way around and *you* were the slave. Would you find it so acceptable then?"

Anger flashed in his eyes and he stood to his full height, glaring down at her. "You go too far, human!"

"Go on then, hit me." Her lips curled back into a snarl, but she refused to back down even though he was larger. Just one punch and that would be it. She didn't care though. Let him try, she'd go down fighting. Maybe quickly but it would be fighting. "Do whatever you want. I'm a slave, remember? No choice, no opinion. Nothing other than a soft body to fuck. Not like we've got brains to use, now is it?"

"Karryl..." Tarrick's voice snapped out in warning, and the temperature in the room dropped several degrees. Karryl flopped into his seat, his expression unreadable, and Tarrick transferred his attention to Cat. Great, she'd pissed off the big-bad.

"Go to my quarters, wait for me there."

"Yes, my *lord*." She mock-saluted him, spun on her heel with a satisfying swish of her skirts and swept out of the door. A sliding door meant she couldn't slam it, so she settled for strutting away with her head held high. Two bots peeled off to escort her, with metallic clicks against the deck plating, as she did her best to storm down the corridor in soft sandals.

Asshole aliens, the lot of them.

LAARN BLEW out a breath after the human woman left the room and broke the silence.

"Anyone else think they're a lot more like us than we bargained for?"

"Seems that way, yes." Tarrick sighed and shook his head. It had been less than a day since they'd taken the base and already he was realizing dealing with humans was fraught with headache. His.

"Okay, Karryl, try and get the women in the cells calm. And leave them in there for now. Until Fenriis arrives with his war group. I don't want the men distracted."

"Huh, just you then?" Laarn, as always, got the jibe in at light speed. "And just how did your night with the little human go? I see she's dressed as befits the mate of a war commander. She accepted your claim, I take it?"

Tarrick clenched his fists, resisting the urge to strangle his brother. He had a point though. They'd all been without women for far too long. To have them just within reach but not be able to touch them would be utter torture.

"Explain that we have to quarantine them for the moment, to ensure their health and safety." Just the mention of a threat to the women's health would have his men toeing the line, no matter how eager they were to claim one for themselves. "Laarn, run full level tests on them to make sure they are all fit and well. That should placate the warriors."

"Of course." His twin's eyes gleamed at the

prospect of being able to gather more data on the new species. Tarrick shook his head. Sometimes he didn't think Laarn was male in the traditional sense of the word.

"The rest of you, back to your stations. I want full level readiness drills run in case the humans arrive before Fenriis. Dismissed."

The warriors filed out, but Tarrick remained in place. Dropping his head back, he closed his eyes for a second in frustration.

They were ready to move onto the next target, the next base in the chain. All the information they'd gathered showed it was larger than the base the humans had designated Sentinel Five. Larger meant more women. More spoils. But they couldn't move yet, not without ships to secure the sector.

But he couldn't hope to hold the entire area with just one war group. It meant bringing in another war commander, his cousin Fenriis, and sharing any spoils the sector might yield, but that was preferable to losing the lot to another clan. It had happened before, and it would happen again. But not this time. Not on his watch.

But first, he had another problem.

Pushing off from the table, he left the briefing room and headed toward his quarters. The two bots he'd assigned to Cat stood in the corridor. He nodded to them as he passed, his thoughts filled with the woman within.

His little human. His little Cat.

As soon as he entered the room, her scent surrounded him. Exotic, erotic, and familiar, all at the same time. She stood in the main room, by the window again. He drank in the sight of her, all sensual curves and softness. Her uniform was gone, replaced by the traditional robes of a Latharian woman.

Gray silk clung to her curves, jeweled straps twinkling on delicate shoulders. The garment dipped low at the back to show the sensual curve of her spine. Jeweled clips held up her hair away from her neck, and bangles glittered on her narrow wrists. Not finery from the K'Vass family vault, just generic ornamentation. It was all he had. He couldn't wait to take her home though, and dress her in the starlight sapphires that had marked his family for centuries.

Unbidden, the image of his mother's bonding necklace flashed through his mind. It was in the family vault, nestled on midnight silk. The most ornate piece of jewelry a latharian woman owned, bonding necklaces were intricate and detailed. His mother's had been modeled after Herris Blossom's, wrought in tri-pladium and set with sapphires. When she wore it, the jeweled flowers looked almost alive against her skin. They would look even more alive against the almost translucent, non-latharian ivory of Cat's skin.

He knew she was aware of his presence from the slight intake of her breath and the stiffness that invaded her limbs. She didn't look at him. Every line of her slender figure radiated tension.

"What was that about?" Crossing the room, he gripped her arm and turned her around to face him. She ignored the pull and yanked her arm free, leaving red marks from his fingers.

"What was what about?" Turning with all the grandeur of an Empress, she gave him an innocent, yet haughty expression. "Back there? Just the truth. Sorry if it hurts."

"You're sad." The realization startled him. Reaching out, he tugged a strand of her hair loose and wound it around his finger. He loved her hair. The vibrant color and the feel of it against his skin was like silk. A sensual delight he hadn't expected. "Why are you sad?"

"Oh, for fuck's sake. You can't be that dense, surely?"

She tried to pull the lock of hair loose, but he

held on. A short tussle ensued, one that ended when he slid his free hand around the nape of her neck and tilted her head. The delicate bones of her neck felt so fragile in his large, warriors hand. He gentled his grip and leaned in to kiss her, heat simmering in his veins, but she bared her teeth in warning.

"I thought we were past all this resistance."

"We are?" She blinked at him, her lips pursed into a stubborn little pout. He wanted to lean down and kiss it away. "No, that would have been the fact you drugged me. It's worn off. Otherwise, I'd have been climbing those warriors in your office like a tree."

He sighed, and closed his eyes for a second. Damn stubborn humans.

"Ker'ann doesn't work like that, little Moore Cat. It eases...the differences between our physical sizes, but it can't create something that's not there." He opened his eyes again. "And this...between us? It is there. Any idiot can see you find me attractive."

"Asshole. I think I like the healer more. He kinda looks like you..."

Anger flared without warning. His hand tightened in her hair. She squeaked, her face paling and he eased his grip again.

"Never look at Laarn again." Jealousy dictated his

responses. The thought of her in another man's arms triggered a rage so deep it scared him. "The only man you should look at is me."

"Whoa, whoa...calm down, big boy." She stroked her hands over his forearms. Her touch was like cool water after the heat of the Arakaas deserts he'd visited as a boy. "I was joking."

"Don't."

The order was short and sharp before he pulled her into his embrace. His mouth had barely covered hers before she tore away.

"No!"

Pulling back, he looked down at her. "No? Why no? We are compatible...you accepted my claim over you."

"Not like I had much choice, did I?" Her voice was sharp and her eyes glittered with angry tears. Why did the sight of them make his chest ache?

"You took mine away to give them theirs. Not that they have much of a choice. Fuck a warrior or become a whore. Did it *ever* occur to you that humanity has been looking for other advanced races? That human women might find you guys attractive and come voluntarily?"

He stilled, his expression setting into unreadable

lines. She'd called him out. He hadn't considered that.

Shoving at his shoulder, she demanded. "You didn't, did you? You just barged right in with bigger guns and took what you wanted."

He shrugged. "It's always been the Lathar way."

"Well, the Lathar are idiots," she huffed. "You're an idiot."

He ventured a small smile. "It's been said before. Laarn still maintains I was dropped on my head at birth."

"Huh. Makes sense."

Sensing a thawing in her attitude, he leaned down to brush his lips over hers. She didn't move or respond. He didn't like her lack of response. Humans were far more complicated than he'd first thought. Last night had been filled with passion and a responsiveness he'd never imagined before and he wanted more. She hadn't pushed him away though, that was something. Under Latharian law, he was more than within his rights to take what he wanted, but he found he didn't want that. He wanted her to open up to him, to give herself. To him.

She lifted her chin. As a signal, it was tiny, but he had nothing else to go on, so grasped it like a lifeline.

He didn't push, instead seducing her with soft

touches and kisses. His lips learned the shape of hers, teasing at the corners, all his senses alert for any reaction from her. She relaxed, a slight weight against him and he eased her closer. She fit into his arms so perfectly that it had to be by design. The ancestors had to have designed her just for him. There was no other explanation.

Tilting her head back farther, he flicked the tip of his tongue against her full lower lip, then teased at it with a slight nip. She gasped, her lips parting. *Softly, softly*, he warned himself, not rushing in as he would have before. When she didn't close them all the way, he kissed her again, stroking his tongue against the parted seam in a request for access.

Her response was a small moan and then she kissed him back. Triumph and relief hit hard and fast. A rumble of need and pleasure in the back of his throat, he deepened the kiss. Tasting her again was as good as his memory, wiping out all other thought. All that mattered was the two of them, her touch, as the rest of the universe whirled around them with a rapid beeping sound.

She pulled away, frowning. "What is that noise? It sounds like an alarm."

He blinked, shook his head and focused.

"Fuck. It's the red alert."

6

*C*at had to trot to keep up with Tarrick as he headed to the bridge. The low-level lighting in the corridor flashed red in rhythmic pulses. Warriors scattered as Tarrick stormed through, parting like the seas before him. She followed in his wake, slipping onto the bridge beside him. Her breath caught in her throat when all the combat bots turned at their entrance, arms spread and talons extended as they focused on her and Tarrick.

Oh shit... Fear crawled down her spine at the memory of their sharp claws. They wouldn't make mincemeat of their own commander...would they? He didn't seem worried. Instead, he paused for half a second before a gleam washed over the surface of the octagonal pendant he wore. Interesting, it seemed their necklaces were less jewelry and more identification. Like a dog tag. She filed that nugget of information away and stayed close as he strode to the center of the bridge.

The central view screen in front of them flickered to life and she sucked in a hard breath. There were more ships now, but these weren't the same design as Tarrick's ships. Black metal glimmered in the light of this system's sun, and weaponry, or what she assumed were weapon arrays, bristled on all surfaces.

"Sheilds to full. Are those T'Laat clan ships?" Tarrick's voice was sharp and cut through the noise on the bridge. "Who heads T'Laat now?"

Cat tucked herself in by an empty console just behind Tarrick and kept quiet. So far, her presence had been accepted but she didn't want to call attention to herself and be taken back to Tarrick's quarters. The more she saw, the more information she could gather. Never knew what could come in handy.

Jassyn looked up from a console on the opposite side of the bridge. From what she could work out, he appeared to be the latharian equivalent of the tactical officer; one trained in strategy and tactics.

"Varish T'Laat."

Silence fell over the bridge at the name. It was a telling silence. Whoever this Varish was, no one liked him much.

"*Draanth!*" Tarrick swore, his tone dropping to a growl. "That changes things."

"Incoming call from the T'Laat flagship, the *Jeru'tias*. Looks like they want to talk," another warrior announced, his hands flying over the console in front of him.

Cat eyed hers with interest. She had always been good with computers. Perhaps she could switch hers on and get a peek at their system. Waving her hand over it did nothing, neither did touching it. The surface only lit up when she put her hand flat on it. Jumping, she yanked her hand back, but the imprint remained in bright blue. Words scrolled across the screen.

Unknown operator, please present identification...

It flickered once, then her handprint disappeared to be replaced by an octagonal outline. She blinked. Okay, so the pendants could access the computer systems. Today's little outing was proving more fruitful by the minute.

"Stall the transmission. Use interference from the human systems." Tarrick was still talking, rattling off orders in quickfire sentences. "Someone put out a call to Fenriis. See how far away his war group is. We will need backup here. I don't trust Varish."

"Accessing the human comms relays." A warrior closer to the view screen kept up a running commentary. "Boosting to full power."

"Got it. No, wait..." Jassyn flicked his hair back over his shoulders and frowned at his screen. "Oh for fuck's sake, it's this bloody repeater pattern again. Can you shut it down, Talat?"

"Yeah, cleaning now. There you go..."

Tarrick prowled the central part of the bridge as his warriors worked, his gaze on the view screen. It was as though she wasn't even there, which suited her fine. She could study him without him being aware.

That he knew what he was doing was obvious. An aura of command surrounded him; unmistakable and sexy. For a moment her lips tingled, reminded of the gentle and oh-so-seductive kiss he'd treated her to before they were interrupted. A kiss she shouldn't have given into. Where had the asshole alien gone? She could handle him, compartmentalize to complete her mission, but when he acted all nice... fuck. She'd be screwed.

No falling for the alien, she told herself. *He's an asshole and you're his slave. Remember that.*

"Bring group configuration to *hanrat-five-nine*," Tarrick ordered, hands clasped behind his back in the classic at-ease position. Huh, seemed certain things crossed not only cultures but galaxies and species too. "Are their weapon arrays active?"

His words brought her attention to the nasty looking canons on the other ships. She assumed they were canons anyway. The basic design didn't seem to differ much from human models. Still a barrel to fire whatever nastiness at the enemy. From what she'd seen, the Lathar used energy-based weapons.

"Powering up. They outgun us."

Shit, this was serious. Cat's lips moved as she counted the canons facing them. If Tarrick's ships were of a similar configuration, then yeah, they were outnumbered. And if this lot were worse than Tarrick's group...fuck. Better the devil you knew.

"Use the base's weaponry," she lifted her voice so it carried. Tarrick pivoted to spear her with a hard gaze.

"What?"

She met his look. "Give me access to the base's mainframe. With the weapon arrays, you'll have a better chance against...those." She waved her hand toward the opposing war group.

"She's right," Jassyn commented, not looking at her, his hands busy on his console. "They're crude but have a decent yield. Our shields took a hammering from them yesterday. Firing systems are...well, unique. We can't figure out how to work them at the moment. Been trying to crack them since yesterday, so yes, if she gives us access, we have the advantage."

"Try nothing," he warned her, striding over and accessing the console with swift gestures.

"Not trying anything other than helping to save your asses. Come on, log me in so I can give you access."

"There, you're in."

Sure enough, the screen flared to life but rather than the alien system, she found herself in the base's familiar mainframe.

She input the access codes for the weaponry and gave the Lathar access.

Ladies, forgive me.

"THANK YOU," Tarrick said, watching his little human out of the corner of his eye. That he was surprised at her offer of help was an understatement, but he would not turn down an advantage like extra weaponry. Not against an enemy as dangerous as Varish. He half expected her to try something, like accessing the weapon arrays and turning them on the K'Vass ships. Something. But she didn't. As soon as she'd granted direct access she stepped away from the console, her hands raised.

"Done, all yours."

"I'm in," Jassyn announced. "Powering up."

"Response from Fenriis," Gaarn called out. "Still over half a pasec away."

Tarrick kept his disappointment to himself. Even at top speed, that meant they couldn't rely on reinforcements.

"Okay, we're doing this solo. Take us to combat status but cut the red alert warnings in this room. Activate all bots for possible boarding parties. If I know Varish, he'll want not only the base but extra ships as spoils."

The Lathar comprised of loosely related war-clans, but there was never any family loyalty lost or mourned. If Varish could defeat them, he would, and claim both the human women and Tarrick's ships once he and all his warriors were dead.

He slid a quick glance at Cat. No emotion showed on her face, her manner calm and serene. His heart twisted at the thought of what would happen to her should Varish and his warriors prevail. He'd given her and her women a choice but Varish T'Laat wouldn't. They'd be claimed and bedded within hours, willing or not.

Taking a deep breath, he nodded to Jassyn. "Put him on the screen."

The view screen flickered for a moment then shifted from a view of the opposing war group to that of a tall, dark-featured warrior. Like Tarrick, he wore the leather and red sash of a War Commander, its edges shot through with gold. Unlike Tarrick, he hadn't cut his warrior's braids, his hair over his shoulders. A new commander but a dangerous one.

"T'Laat." Tarrick inclined his head, a show of respect between those of equal rank. "To what do we owe the pleasure?"

"Can a warrior not check in with a kinsman now, without his motives being suspect?" Varish smiled. It was the oily, slick smile of a politician, one that all

Tarrick's instincts warned him not to trust. How the hell had Varish found them? His warriors knew the score. They knew not to talk about their missions, not even at the pleasure stops, and there was no way to track the ships.

Out of Varish's line of sight, Jassyn coughed. *"Trall-shit."*

Tarrick kept his expression neutral. Varish could use anything, even a flicker of an eyelid, and he'd be damned if he would give the rival warrior anything to work with.

"Your concern is noted."

Varish's smile widened. "And to offer my help with your current situation."

Ah, now they got down to it. Tarrick offered a smile just as empty and false as Varish's own.

"Thank you, but we have things quite in hand."

"Really? Looks like a big sector here... plenty for everyone." Varish moved to the side, his gaze focusing on Cat behind Tarrick. "You have found females?"

"A handful." Tarrick folded his arms. There was no way Varish's scanners could pick up the women in the holding cells, not through the *Velu'vais's* shields. "The species in this sector appear to have the same problem as we have. Few women, even less fertile."

"A few females is better than none." Varish leaned back, a smug expression on his face. "Since this sector falls within my established remit, you will cede all captured women. At once."

Tarrick heard the slight intake of breath behind him but couldn't turn to assure Cat that Varish's words held no weight. One did not look away from a snake lest it strike.

"Your established remit? I suggest you double check the records," he advised. "This area falls under K'Vass space."

"Ahh, it *did*," Varish looked so smug Tarrick wanted to reach through the screen and splatter that long nose all over his face. "Before I submitted a requisition with the emperor's recordkeepers. And..." he spread his hands. "I appear to have the advantage of superior numbers here. And don't think for a moment I can't see you've activated the weaponry on that primitive little station there."

Tarrick stared back. "Marginally superior numbers, but it will make no difference. This is K'Vass space and we protect our own. Do you want to start something you can't finish, Varish? Because I assure you we'll send you packing with your tail between your legs."

Varish smiled again. "With those ships and one little base? With the looks of the technology, I'm surprised it's even holding its orbit. I'll tell you what, Tarrick, given our kinship, I will give you one hour to think it through. Then you *will* cede the females or your bloodline will end here."

SHITSHITSHIT.

Only an idiot wouldn't have realized that the situation was serious and Cat was far from a fool. Tension rolled around the bridge during Tarrick's conversation with the other alien lord, the reactions of the warriors too careful and controlled. But it wasn't until he cut the communication she realized just *how* serious it was.

"Lock down all comms channels," he ordered as soon as the screen went blank. "And someone get me a direct line with the emperor. I want this shit sorted out *now!*"

He turned, gaze locking on hers and she swallowed. If she'd thought he looked dangerous before, it was nothing compared to the lethal aura that surrounded him now. He stalked toward her, intent written into every movement and swept her up into his embrace.

She bit her lower lip, allowing him to pull her close. Events were moving fast. So fast her head whirled. This morning it had been so simple. All she'd had to figure out was how to liberate just under a hundred women from the clutches of sex-mad aliens, find a ship, and pilot a course back to the safety of human-held space.

Oh yeah, and warn them that sexy, ripped aliens from the outer reaches of spaces were out there looking for women to capture and bed.

Okay, scratch that...If women on Earth saw what the Lathar looked like, they'd leave in droves in anything spaceworthy.

With this though, things changed. Now she had a whole new set of aliens to deal with and if she'd thought Tarrick's lot were assholes, Varish appeared to up the ante to total bastard.

"You won't let him take us?" she asked. Despite herself, her strong woman mask slipped a little and she clung to him. She had to be realistic. He might be her captor, but so far he hadn't lifted a finger against her, even earlier when she'd resisted. Instead, he'd seduced her with soft kisses.

Something she doubted the cruel-faced Varish would have done. A shiver worked its way down her spine as she recalled the way he'd looked at her like he was mentally undressing her. She felt sick, unclean, at the thought.

"No, my love. I won't." The endearment slipped from his lips and warmed her heart even though she tried to stop it. "You're mine and the K'Vass protect what is theirs."

He bent his head and claimed her lips in a blazing kiss. She moaned, pressing herself against him, but it was over too soon. Pulling back, he looked down at her, smiled and stroked her cheek. "Karryl will take you down to the others while I'm in council with the emperor. You'll be well protected, I promise."

When Tarrick had said the women would be well protected, he'd meant it. Within minutes, Cat was ushered into the main holding area within the bowels of the ship. The force field for the cell snapped into place behind her and the robotic guard whirled away to resume its patrol. She turned and was overwhelmed as the women in the cell rushed her.

"Oh my god, are you okay?"

"What happened?"

"Can you tell us what's going on?"

The voices rose in a babble of questions, almost deafening her. She didn't know which to answer first. She was saved as another voice broke through, the tone commanding.

"Oh, for heaven's sake, leave the poor girl alone."

Cat breathed a sigh of relief as a familiar figure barged her way through the mass of bodies to stand next to her. Major Jane Allen had been the senior female officer aboard Sentinel Five and a Marine. Now, with the loss of the captain and the other men, she was the senior officer overall.

"Ma'am," Cat muttered by way of thanks. At least now she could ease off for a moment. She wasn't alone, Major Allen had years more experience than she did and tactical training only Marines received. Not just that, but she was the Fleet's poster girl for military service, a legend who looked far younger than her years. Some said living space side did that.

"Glad to have you back, Moore." The major reached out to squeeze Cat's upper arms, bared by the alien outfit she wore. A quick reassuring gesture. Cat spared a quick glance to look through the faces, trying to spot Jess but couldn't. Damn, she must be in one of the other cells.

Major Allen reclaimed her attention. "What can you tell us?"

"So, they're bigger versions of us?"

Cat, seated in a small circle with the other women in the cell, nodded. "Yes. There doesn't appear to be any physical difference, just the size. I can't tell you about the inner workings of their bodies but on the outside, they look like human men, just bigger."

"Bigger, huh?" One woman the other side of the circle sniggered and Cat flushed.

"Enough of that," Major Allen, Jane, reproached. "Focus on the issue at hand. So, they're bigger, they appear to have a feudal society that uses energy-based weaponry and these remote-operated bot creatures. What else?"

"They have no women." At Cat's revelation, all the ladies turned to her. She shrugged. "What did you think when we were separated from the men? Apart from the obvious?"

"Well, sex slaves were an obvious when they started the segregation," Jane commented, her expression grim. "So we have a ship full of horny alien warriors here. I'm surprised they left us alone this long."

Cat looked down at her hands. Crap, crunch time.

"I made a deal," she whispered. "They have an honor-based system. They didn't take us for one-night stands. They respect and revere women. With none of their own, they look for women to capture... then claim. Seems to be one warrior, one woman."

"Just one?" Someone chuckled. "Damn, and there I was looking forward to a hunky alien threesome."

"Yeah, right, Kenna...you'd eat them for breakfast. Hey, perhaps that's it. We send Kenna out there and they'll all run screaming."

The group dissolved into chuckles. Cat smiled, sitting back. It was such a relief to talk, even shooting the shit like this. She wasn't alone anymore, didn't have to make all the big decisions. That no one judged her like she worried they would was a weight off her shoulders. But then, with the Sentinel bases being so far out on the frontier, all personnel were military. They knew the score. If the shit hit the fan, the military mindset kicked in.

"On the whole, they're decent people. They have an honor code," she carried on. "I mean, look at us... we did the whole slavery thing ourselves, and we didn't give them a single choice, never mind three."

"Three choices? Of men, right?" Jane asked, her brow furrowed.

Cat nodded. "That's right. You don't have to say yes to the first warrior who puts in a claim. You can say no up to three times."

"What happens then?"

Cat's expression dropped. "Sent to the brothels. I'd suggest no one get to that point."

From the grim looks around her, they all agreed.

"Sounds like we need to consider this from a tactical viewpoint," Jane said quietly, turning to look at Cat. "But first I want to know about this deal you made."

She shrugged. "It's not a big thing. I didn't agree to anything for anyone else..."

"Cat?" Jane's hand closed over hers, battle-scarred but gentle all the same. "What did you agree to?"

She looked up and met the other woman's eyes. They were odd; one green, one blue. Huh. She'd never noticed that.

"Tarrick...their lord, the one in charge..." She paused and closed her eyes, her words escaping in a rush. "If I agreed to his claim over me, then the rest of you got the choices."

There was silence. Complete and utter silence.

Cat cracked one eyelid, then another and looked around. Sadness and approval shimmered in Jane's eyes, echoed on the faces of the other women. Jane squeezed her hands.

"Thank you. That was a noble sacrifice. He didn't...he wasn't..."

"No." Cat was quick to shake her head. "No, not at all. I mean...there's something they inject into you—"

"The bastard drugged you?" This time it was Kenna who spoke up, her voice outraged. "When I see him, I'm gutting him. With a fucking blunt spoon."

"It's not like that. It...well, they're bigger than us. *Way* bigger. The stuff makes you dilate...down there. You know. You feel buzzed and all, but it's like two shots of decent vodka."

At the word, there were several moans. Supply runs to the base were comprised of essentials, so alcohol was in short supply. Cat had even heard tell someone on one of the lower levels had been trying to distil their own. No one was blind yet, so she assumed it was an "urban" myth or they'd managed it.

"We have other problems though," Cat cut through the groaning to bring the conversation back on course. As she did so, she reached out to touch Jane's arm, her finger tapping. Tap or press in quick succession until Jane looked at her, eyes widening a little as she got the message.

They don't understand morse code.

"There's another group of aliens here, they seem to be in a power struggle with this lot."

"Over?" Jane nodded as she spoke, letting Cat know she understood.

The ident tags...

"Us. Women from this sector. The ones who just arrived are mounting a challenge for this area of space. And believe me..." She shuddered. "This lot don't look like they'll give us any choices."

...access the computers.

"Shit. What do we do?" Kenna, another of the Marines, crowded forward, dividing her attention between Jane and Cat. The muscles in her shoulders bunched as she rolled her neck as though preparing for a fight.

Jane looked around, frowning at the sound of a commotion by the door. Before she could answer, energy bolts slammed into the field keeping them in the cell. It fizzled out and disappeared as a bot crashed to the floor in front of them, a smoking hole in the middle of its chest.

"Right now? Run!" Jane bellowed as the fight broke into the room.

The women scattered, streaming out of the holding cells as more robots poured into the room to engage the ones that had been guarding them. The black metal carapaces of the newcomers made them easy to distinguish.

Cat gathered her skirts and ran between the fighting monsters, following Jane's lead. If they could just get into the central section of the vessel, they might make it to the flight deck. Find a ship. Failing that, they could at least access the weapons lockers she'd seen in the corridors.

The black robots had the advantage of numbers though, and before they could escape the room, had all but cut down the others. Cat stifled a scream as a silver-colored robot crashed to its knees in front of her, saved from being crushed when Kenna grabbed her hand and yanked her back.

"To the left," she yelled and a black robot whirled around to fix its single red eye on them. "Go, go, go!"

She pushed Cat ahead of her, both of them slipping on grease that oozed from the fallen robot like blood leaking from ruined veins. Her breath escaped in a squeak, Cat righted herself but felt Kenna yanked from her grasp. She glanced back over her shoulder to see the Marine woman in the clutches of a black robot.

"*Run!*" Kenna yelled, fighting to escape its clutches. Although its talons dripped with the "blood" of the bots it had destroyed, it folded the lethal blades away so they didn't cut the struggling woman. Looked like they were the same as Tarrick's bots, they wouldn't kill them...but she wouldn't hang around. As long as one woman got away, there was hope for the rest.

She spun on her heel and sprinted for the open doors. Metal flashed in her peripheral vision, the robots reaching out to grab her. All black now, there were no silver ones left on their feet. Bellowing, she ducked and wove, trying to escape their grasp. Her heart pounded in her chest, powering the muscles of her body in her desperate bid for escape. Just ahead of her was Jane, the other woman's lithe form and fitness more suited for a pitched battle against alien combat robots. Shit.

It made no difference. Before either of them

reached the doors, two heavier-set black robots stepped in the way. Their eyes focused on the two women and both skidded to a halt as red dots appeared on their chests. Slowly, they raised their hands in the universal symbol for surrender.

"So much for not killing women," Jane shrugged. "I can't believe I'm saying this... Okay, asshole. Take us to your leader."

7

*A*s evil alien overlords went, Varish T'Laat ticked all the boxes and then some. He wore the same uniform as Tarrick, right down to the red sash, but the leather was darker and battered. Extra sections of sewn-in armor made him look more sinister and the vicious scar down one side of his face just by his eye didn't help him much in the approachable and cuddly stakes.

The women were herded to stand in front of him in a large room. Long and high-ceilinged, it resembled a throne room. An impression that was aided because Varish sat on a damn throne. He leaned forward, dark hair falling across eyes so cold that Cat shivered.

"Who is in charge here?" His voice was silky

smooth. Although they should know better, a few of the women glanced toward Jane near the front of the group.

She stepped forward, chin high as she looked Varish in the eye. "That would be me. Major All—"

In a move like lightning, he pulled the heavy pistol and fired. Jane cried out, clutching her leg as she collapsed on the floor. Cat gasped, her immediate instinct to go to the fallen woman, but Varish motioned with the pistol.

"Correction. *I* am in charge." He stood, heavy boots clumping against the steps as he descended the dais. When he reached Jane, he looked down at the fallen woman as she panted in pain, her forehead pressed against the floor. No sympathy showed in his expression. Then he looked up at the rest of them.

"You belong to the T'Laat now. And you have two choices."

None of the women responded with so much as a murmur. They were all too wary to risk a response that would get them all shot.

"Good, you're learning already." Varish smiled, walking around the small group with a measured tread and praising them like he would a puppy that had mastered a new trick. "Either you behave or you suffer. Simple as that. I'm not K'Vass... your sole purpose aboard this ship is to offer comfort for my men."

He paused in front of them, caressing the barrel of the pistol in a very unhealthy manner. "Remember that you do not have to look pretty, or even be able to move, for them to use your soft cunts. Do you understand?"

No response. There never would be to a declaration like that.

"Good." He clicked his fingers at Cat. "You... K'Vass's woman. Come here."

A chill swept over her skin, but she took a step forward, then another, forcing her unwilling body to approach him. Every instinct within her urged her to run, to get as far away from him as she could as fast as she could but she knew it wasn't possible. He'd cut her down before she'd taken three steps and would laugh as she died in agony.

She came to a stop in front of him, her eyes on the floor. Not the modesty of a slave faced with her master but pure self-preservation. If he looked into her eyes, he'd see she wanted to gut him. Slowly.

"I can see why K'Vass chose you. You are lovely." He reached out and ran a hand down the exposed length of her arm, strong fingers shackling her wrist and he pulled her up against him. Revulsion filled her, bile rising in her throat as strong arms wrapped around her. Cat scratched at his neck and shoulders, doing no harm to the battered leather but using the movement to cover as she snapped the chain around his neck. She tore free of his grasp and stepped backward.

His face contorted in fury and he lashed out, backhanding her across the face. Pain flared in her cheek and she spun around, stumbling as she fell onto Jane on the floor.

"Bitch!" he hissed, standing over her. "Never, *never* say no. Ever!"

"I'm sorry, my Lord," Cat sobbed noisily, keeping her hand concealed beneath her body as she pressed Varish's ident tag into Jane's hands. The other woman, lips still pressed together in pain, gave an almost imperceptible nod.

"You'd better be," he snarled, wrapping a hard hand around her upper arm and hauling her bodily to her feet. "Get the rest of them prepared for the choosing ceremony," he ordered the guards, already dragging Cat from the room. "Leave that one there until it dies. As a warning."

He said nothing more. Instead, he stormed from the room, dragging Cat in his wake. She didn't try to pry his fingers from her arm, knowing that the reprisal was likely to be deadly.

"Please, my Lord. I'm sorry," she whined, keeping up the pretense of a panicked slave. All the while though, she kept an eye out for something, anything she could use.

Hopefully, the throne room would be cleared and Jane allowed to move freely. If she were able. Cat had been in the computer core then unconscious for most of the Lathar attack on the base so she had no idea how bad injuries from those pistols could be. The Marine had been conscious, at least. And conscious was good, right? It meant they had a chance.

"You will be," he muttered as they reached the end of a corridor and a door swished open in front of them. Unlike Tarrick's, which were neat and military-sparse, Varish's quarters were opulent and decadent.

He shoved her into a large room. She had a fleeting impression of large couches and sumptuous rugs before he pushed her into a bedroom. Her mouth dropped open. It looked as though it had been pulled from a bad romance holo-movie she'd once seen, *the Space Sultan's Harem*.

There was already someone there, a tall, slender

woman wearing robes in the corner of the room. Cat sucked in a breath. Was Varish into voyeurism as well?

"Out!" He barked the order at the other woman, who slipped past them without a word of complaint.

Cat got a look under her hood at her face as she did so. It was a long face, not human or lathar looking at all but more like a human version of a cow. The creature scuttled out before Cat could say a word.

He pulled her around to face him, her back to the bed and looked down at her. He was as well built as Tarrick was, and he was handsome, even with the scar, but she felt nothing other than a mixture of anger and fear.

"You're a pretty one," he mused, as though he were talking to himself. Like she wasn't even present...or didn't matter. Given his words earlier, she was going with *didn't matter*. She tried not to flinch as he reached out and touched her cheek. A gentle touch, now. She doubted it would stay so.

"I can see what K'Vass saw in you. It will kill him to know I've got you now...that it's my cock buried in your silken depths. Plowing you over and over until you scream my name."

"I'll never scream your name," she promised and

struck. He was so close he couldn't block and a man was a man all over the galaxy. Even the Lathar kept their balls between their legs, just like humans. Bringing her knee up, she clocked him hard in the groin.

He grunted, folding at the waist. She tried to slide to the side, escape him, but his hand shot out and grabbed her arm in a punishing grip. Screaming, she fought like a wildcat, landing blows where ever she could. It made no difference. Straightening up, he backhanded her again, the power of the blow knocking her backward over the bed. On her in an instant, he pinned her to the soft surface with his body, the bulge in his groin pressing hard against her.

"I didn't say you'd be screaming in pleasure, did I?"

THE LATHARIAN EMPEROR was the greatest warrior in their culture, a man both revered and feared as the physical embodiment of the ancestor gods. He was also Tarrick's uncle, on his mother's side. Family connections didn't mean that Tarrick could duck out of a holo-connection with the man early though, not even with a red alert ringing in his ears.

"Thank you, Imperial Majesty," he murmured, bending into a low bow. Light years away his "body," a non-combat avatar, bowed before the Emperor as he swept from the room, followed by his entourage. Tarrick curled his lip at the soft-bodied, useless courtiers, safe in the knowledge the bot didn't have the facial muscles to pick up the movement. Straightening, he brought the bot back to a stable position and released his hold on it.

Instantly, he was back on an uplink couch in the pilots lounge. Tearing the headset off, he looked up. Other recliners surrounded him in rows. They were all occupied, each warrior wearing an identical headset to remotely pilot the avatars.

A yell from the other side of the room made his head snap around. A warrior fell from his couch, tearing his headset off as he went. "Fuck, avatar down! There are too many of them."

"What the hell is going on?" he demanded, levering himself up and handing his headset off to the warrior hovering next to him. Before the impression of his body had smoothed from the padded surface of the couch, the other man slid onto it and put the headset on, the visor covering his eyes.

A second later, lights flashed active on the front, the red and blue lights showing a local link rather than the subspace link Tarrick had used.

"The T'Laat attacked," Jassyn, waiting by the door, informed him. "Hit us hard and fast...took the women. They're fighting a ferocious rear-guard action that's slowing us."

Tarrick froze as fear lanced the center of his chest and his body forgot to breathe. Varish T'Laat had Cat. The thought of his little human in that monster's clutches... He gritted his teeth. Varish's reputation preceded him. Ruthless and determined in battle, he was sadistic and vicious in more intimate pursuits. So much so, most pleasure facilities refused to take his credit. Only those that catered to specific...tastes would allow him and his men entry.

"How much time?" he demanded, marching past Jassyn. "They'll have taken them back to the flagship. Do we still have that hunter-seeker program on lockdown from the B'Kaar?"

"Yes, my Lord. Want me to break it out?"

Tarrick nodded. Although most Lathar clans focused on militaristic pursuits, some, like the B'Kaar, specialized in different forms of warfare. The B'Kaar took digital and subspace combat to the highest level. A hunter-seeker program had cost Tarrick a lot of credits, but he'd never had cause to use it. The prospect of losing Cat though meant he was prepared to put all his cards on the table.

"I don't care how you do it, but get me onto that ship. They are not keeping our women."

Jassyn nodded, heading for his console on the bridge as soon as they cleared the doors. All Tarrick's senior warriors were present, and Karryl threw a blast assault rifle his way. Tarrick didn't slow his pace, catching it mid-air. "Jassyn, you coordinate from here. Gaarn, power up a *Kelaas* assault flyer."

"Already done, my Lord. It's waiting on the flight deck," the pilot confirmed, falling into step behind Tarrick and Karryl.

"Now, let's get our women back."

THE FLIGHT between the two ships was short. Barely had they left the flight deck of the *Velu'vias* than Gaarn had settled the small assault flyer on the hull of Varish's flagship. The hull cutter hit metal with a clunk and cut through the tri-plated covering with a squeal. Through the flyer's viewscreen, Tarrick watched other units touchdown, the bigger, hulking forms of the bot transports between them. Impatience made him shift from foot to foot and anger tensed his body until his vision faded to red at the edges.

"Easy, boss." Karryl dropped a big hand on Tarrick's shoulder, his expression both sympathetic and concerned. "We'll get them back, I promise. Just think, they're confusing the fuck out of that lot right now."

"Yeah, ain't that the truth." Unbidden a smile curved Tarrick's lips.

The human women were the most contrary creatures he'd ever come across; fascinating and frustrating by equal terms. But he knew just as well as Karryl that spirit could be crushed under a Lathar fist. They'd already had the women for hours...he bit back a growl. Who knew what they'd been subjected to.

"We're through." The shout came from the back of the flyer. Like a well-oiled machine, the Lathar warriors formed an attack formation and swarmed through the blown hatchway into an empty corridor. Empty was good, it meant either the ship's internal defenses were offline or engaged elsewhere.

"K'Vass here," Tarrick spoke, triggering his

comms line. "We are boots on deck. Confirm hunter-seeker program active."

The comm line crackled and Jassyn's voice filled his ear. "Active and in their system, sir. Half their bots down. Others on a different codex. Working on them."

Farther down the corridor, more of Tarrick's men poured through similar boarding holes, followed by the metal combat avatars. He watched as they organized themselves into a slick, well-practiced march of death, and moved farther into the ship toward their objectives.

"No resistance so far." He kept up the running commentary as he and his men made their way down the empty corridors toward the center of the ship. Varish would be on the bridge, or—Tarrick didn't want to think about it, but he had to—he'd be in his quarters.

With Cat.

At the thought of his little Cat in the vile warrior's arms, fury threatened to rise and overwhelm him again. Tarrick fought it, his eyes narrowing as they approached the central hall of the ship and heard sounds of combat from around the next corner.

"Jass...do we have units this far in?" he asked, his

blast rifle tucked into his shoulder, ready to fire. They were the only group on this boarding vector and their time had been fast. It was unlikely another combat team had gotten ahead of them.

"No. All other units are at least a kilisec behind you."

"Okay..." Tarrick lifted his hand from the trigger grip and gave rapid-fire combat signals, rearranging his men to turn the corner. A female yell made him pause and blink. There were no female Lathar warriors...

"Move!" Tarrick gave the order, and the warriors swarmed around the corners to find a scene they hadn't expected in a million years. A small group of human women held the corridor, bottlenecking the T'Laat combat bots and warriors. Somehow they'd broken into a weapons cache, and were wielding the big assault rifles with an ability and violence that astounded Tarrick.

"Target the joints," a woman near the front bellowed as she stepped out of cover behind a support strut, favoring a leg and took aim. She fired in short, controlled bursts at a bot trying to break through their line, and shattered its knee joints.

"They've taken the thermal safeties offline." Surprise rang in Karryl's voice. It was the only way the big weapons would fire that fast. "They'll kill themselves."

It might be dangerous, but it was damn effective. As was the weird way they fired, in bursts rather than precision single shots to take out the central processors on the bots. The Lathar warriors ran up behind the women, settling into positions beside them.

"About time you boys showed up," the woman controlling the action threw at them as Tarrick and Karryl slid into place next to her. She didn't take her eyes off the action ahead of them, continuing to fire until the rifle she held whined.

Tarrick's heart pounded. The rifle was on overload. Both he and Karryl reached out at the same time to snatch the weapon from her hands, but she stood and launched it at the T'Laat warriors, yelling, "Fire in the hole!"

As one, the women turned away, shielding their heads and faces as the whine of the rifle grew to ear-splitting proportions. Tarrick and his men barely had time to throw themselves into cover before it exploded, rendering the approaching avatar bots twisted hunks of metal and leaving the warriors behind either dead or mortally wounded.

"Holy fuck," Karryl breathed the words, but they

were the ones on every K'Vass warriors' mind. "You're...scary."

"He gave us two choices. Slavery or suffering. So we made them suffer." The woman turned and smiled. Tarrick recognized her as the human soldier who had impressed Karryl. Now he could see why.

Her gaze flicked over him and Karryl and he realized she was wounded, a large dressing around her thigh. Reaching around her neck, she unlooped something and held it out to him.

It was an ident tag. Shit, now he knew how they'd gotten into the weapons cache.

"He has Cat. Go get her."

His fingers brushed hers as he took the tag. He nodded, a mark of respect from one warrior to another.

"Thank you."

He took off down the corridor, the chain wrapped around his fist and activated his comm. "Jassyn, locate Varish."

Less than three kilisecs later Tarrick crashed through the outer door into Varish's quarters. An Oonat cowered in the corner, her large, doe-like eyes wide with fear.

"Where?" he demanded, knowing he was scaring

the creature but not able to do anything about it at the moment.

She shrieked, huddled into the corner and pointed toward the bedroom. Tarrick's head whipped around to the door. Shit. They were in...He had Cat in his sleeping chamber.

The inner door was no match for his boot as he kicked it in. What was it with Varish and this archaic décor? They might have been desert nomads way back when but they didn't need to live it now.

"You fucking bitch, you *will* submit." The snarl was punctuated by the sound of a fist hitting soft skin. Varish knelt on the bed, a smaller figure pinned beneath him. The spill of gray silk and human-dark hair were all Tarrick saw before fury overwhelmed him and he launched himself toward the bed with a roar.

at's world had reduced to two things: pain and ensuring her tormentor didn't take her quickly. He wouldn't kill her, not with women in such short supply, but she made sure he wanted to. Death would be a release. The final escape from a situation in which she saw no other way out. And if she were lucky, she could take this asshole's ability to procreate away so he'd never rape another woman.

He roared as he hit her, landing blows when she couldn't block fast enough, but still she fought. And when she couldn't fight anymore, when her arms were too heavy to hold him off, he still roared.

But the blows stopped.

Blessed unconsciousness beckoned and she

welcomed it. She hoped she wouldn't wake, but even if she did, she'd find another way to make sure she escaped him. Permanently.

A different roar filled the room, followed by another and she struggled to open her eyes. What was it? Did the asshole get off on howling like an animal? Large bodies danced in front of her and she squinted to bring them into focus. They stumbled toward her and she gasped, rolling to push herself off the soft surface of the bed. She landed on the floor with a thud and cried out in pain as they fell on the bed where she'd just been.

"I'll kill you for touching her." The snarl was low and almost unrecognizable, but she focused enough to spot Tarrick, his hands around Varish's throat as he throttled him. He'd come for her. Warmth spread through her chest, relief, and something deeper filtering through her bruised body.

She stayed awake as he twisted and dragged Varish off the bed to kneel before him. His eyes met hers as he wrapped a thick arm around Varish's neck and squeezed.

Her eyelids drooped down, only to snap up again when there was commotion at the door. More warriors burst in and fear lanced her gut, but then she relaxed as she focused enough to recognize Tarrick's senior officers.

"Shit...he's got T'Laat."

"Secure the room."

"Where's the woman?"

"Over here...got her."

She shuffled upright, her back to the wall as the warriors swarmed into the room, but her attention was all on Tarrick. His lips curled back in a snarl, he throttled the life out of Varish. The other warrior went purple, hands scrabbling at Tarrick's arms, trying to get him to let go. But Tarrick held firm. Varish's eyes turned back in his head and he jerked, then went limp. Shifting his hold, Tarrick curled back his lips and twisted, snapping the unconscious warriors neck with a sharp crack. The body dropped to his feet in a heap.

She shivered, not able to muster an ounce of sorrow in her heart for the dead alien.

"Well, haven't you gotten yourself into a spot of bother," a voice murmured softly, gentle hands smoothing down her limbs. She turned her head to see Laarn leaning over her, his face, so like her Tarrick's, lined with concern.

"Iz nothi'," she slurred and tried to swallow. Crap, her throat hurt like hell. "A mere flesh woun'."

She laughed, amused she was quoting old movies in a situation as dire as this. Laarn shook his head and pressed something against her throat. Coolness ran through her veins, stealing away her pain.

"Are the others okay?" They had to be if Tarrick and his men were there.

"They're fine... You worry about yourself." Laarn shook his head. "I'll give you this, you humans are damn tough."

"They are," Tarrick knelt on her other side, reaching out to stroke a gentle finger down her cheek. "And this one's the toughest of them all. But what did you expect from a lord's chosen?"

"Careful," Laarn warned as Tarrick slid his arms under her shoulders and knees. "She's badly bruised. A few cracked ribs, but thankfully humans are easy to mend."

She sighed, feeling no pain thanks to the medication as he gathered her into his arms and stood. Just being held by him again was more than she'd hoped for and to her embarrassment, tears leaked onto her cheeks.

"Shhhh, it's over, little one," he murmured, pressing his forehead against hers. For a moment, they just stood there, and she clung to his shoulders as though she could absorb his strength through touch alone.

"I thought I'd lost you. Never do that again, Moore Cat."

"Yeah, I'll pass on the getting kidnaped by aliens thing for a while. Once is fine." She chuckled, wincing a little at the movement. It didn't help that he began to walk, but she didn't argue. The quicker they got off this damn ship, the better.

"I hope not. Since I plan to kidnap you right now."

"You can't kidnap the willing. Don't you know that?" She smiled, closing her eyes and resting her head on his shoulder. He was here, she was safe, and she allowed herself to relax, letting the medication Laarn had given her do its job.

Soon after, she came to and found him carrying her down the corridors of his ship. The sight of the K'Vass avatar bots almost made her cry with relief.

"Never thought I'd be pleased to see those things," she said, looking over his shoulder as he carried her into his quarters. Looking up at his tight expression, she felt awkward and nervous.

"Tarrick?"

He didn't carry her to the bedroom. Instead, he put her on the couch in the main room and knelt before her.

"Moore Cat..." His big hands enveloped hers and when he looked up, the expression in his eyes made her heart stutter. "When we attacked your base, we didn't know about humans. We...you have astonished me. How you work together to defeat the T'Laat. Amazing. Particularly for mere women."

She pressed her lips together, brow arched. "You were doing so well there for a moment. *Mere* women?"

He hissed in frustration, shaking his head. "Old warriors struggle with change. We have no women, we're not used to females with intelligence. The nearest thing we have are the Oonat, and they're more animal-like. Grazers."

Her eyes widened. "Varish had a woman in his rooms. Her face was longer, more like a cow...that's an Earth animal. Also a grazer."

"She was an Oonat." Tarrick nodded, stroking his thumb over the inside of her wrist in a way that made her skin tingle. "They're not very intelligent. Don't even mount a defense when we raid their homeworlds for new females. They are nothing like you."

Lifting his hand, he cupped the side of her face. It was no longer sore, but even with the best medicine in the universe, she knew she looked terrible. The swelling in her body was gone, but her skin was still bruised dark purple so she had no reason to believe her face had faired any better.

"You are remarkable," his voice lowered at the same time his gaze dropped to her lips. He was about to kiss her, she realized, a second before he leaned forward to press a soft kiss against her lips. She murmured, lips clinging to his before he pulled back. "And have made me reassess my opinions on humanity. I have confirmation of the K'Vass clan's claim to this sector of space."

"And? Does that mean you'll be raiding to collect more women?" she asked, tilting her head. "Or have you realized we're more trouble than we're worth?"

His lips quirked. "Sassy creature. You are a lot of trouble."

He looked at her and his expression dropped serious. Her heart fell. They would continue raiding...

"I won't let you go. I *can't* let you go."

The raw admission surprised her, almost as much as his fast move when he swept her into his arms and sat with her in his lap. His lips claimed hers in a rush, his tongue prying them apart to delve within. Heat hit, making her catch her breath and forcing her heart to beat at a rapid pace. His fingers drove into her hair, holding her still as he plundered her mouth with a desperation she'd never sensed in him.

Pressed against him, his body heat inflamed her, matched by the heat that infiltrated her veins. An ache speared her, centered in her pussy as the need to have him touch her, fill her, wiped out her ability to think of anything beyond his next kiss. She'd survived, and that was all that mattered. She needed this, needed the balm of his touch, needed him.

He pulled away, resting his forehead against hers again, his breathing ragged. "I'll let the men go, send out a diplomatic party to your people, but I won't release you, Moore Cat. Never."

She pulled away to look at him in surprise. "So you'll free some of us?"

He nodded. "Just the men. Not the women. My men would lynch me."

"What about the women who don't want to be here? Did you forget the whole kidnap thing? We don't like that, remember? Or would you like to talk to the T'Laat to refresh your memory?"

He groaned, the sound turning into a soft

chuckle. When he looked at her, his gaze was level. "Work with me, Cat. I'm changing centuries of tradition here to give you a choice, okay?"

Slowly, she nodded. He was, she appreciated that. But still... Sliding her hands up his muscled forearms, she played with the short hairs at the base of his neck. "Okay, but I have conditions."

He arched an eyebrow, watching her. His hand swept up the curve of her waist to settle on her ribcage and his thumb stroked the under curve of her bust. It was distracting, and from the slight quirk of his lips, he knew it too.

"No drugs. Never again. For any of us."

He froze for a second, then nodded. "It doesn't work that way, but if it makes you happy, I'll tell Laarn it's not to be used except by the female's request. Happy?"

A smile teased at the edges of her lips and she nodded. He was serious about this whole changing thing. "And if they refuse three times...You send them home. Agreed?"

His eyes widened. "But—"

"A-a-a!" She put her finger to his lips to hush him. "Work with me, or I won't be a happy little Moore Cat. And you want a happy one, don't you?

Or at least one that isn't in your computer system, screwing about with your bots."

As she spoke, she opened her hand, revealing that she'd palmed his ident tag and dangled it in front of him. He swore, reaching for his neck, then smiled. The expression flashed with frustration and fire.

"Damned if I do, and damned if I don't." He sighed. "Okay, three choices, then the ones who are married to human men can return. The others, they must stay and support the claimed women... help us learn about your culture and how to appeal to your females. Do all humans drive such hard bargains?" he grumbled, tilting her head forward to drop a kiss into her hair.

"Harder," she confirmed, shifting her position to straddle him. Her breath escaped in a hiss as she settled and the thick length of his cock pressed right where she needed it. "But if it's harder you want..."

His growl was less frustration and more need as his hands closed over her hips. "Damn humans...I'll give you harder."

"Oh, I hope so."

He had her flipped onto her back in a heartbeat, stretching his big, hard warriors body over her. She was still black and blue from her ordeal on Varish's ship and wore her torn robes, but the look in his eyes said she was the most beautiful thing he'd ever seen.

"When I think of you in danger..." His eyes were so haunted she reached up to cup his cheek as she kissed him. "He didn't—"

"Shhh, it's over. No, he didn't. I'm safe. I'm here, with you." She punctuated each word with a soft kiss. "Please, Tarrick, help me forget. Touch me."

With a growl, he did as asked, sliding his hands up her legs under the gray silks. His mouth covered hers again and the kiss swept her away.

There was no exploration this time, just heat. She didn't care. After defying death or worse, she wanted to feel alive. And she'd never felt more alive as when she was in his arms. Her hands roved over his shoulders and down his biceps before she pulled at his jacket. She needed to touch him. Now.

His tongue brushed against hers in a hot, slick dance. The fastenings of his jacket resisted her and she growled, drawing a soft chuckle from him. He broke away for a moment to draw the zipper down, murmuring against her lips. "Ferocious little Cat."

"Rawr," she replied, and sliding her hands under the leather, dragged her nails up his back.

He gasped, spine arching and his eyes flared gold with heat. Need so intense she felt the burn.

"Mine," he whispered, thumb under her chin forcing her head up so he could kiss her neck. She shivered, loving the feel of his mouth on her. "All mine."

His free hand shoved her gown up past her waist at the same time he slid a knee between her legs. He was still clothed and she was naked beneath the robes, but she didn't care, her hands dropping to the fastenings at his crotch. She needed him with impatience and desperation that bordered on painful.

"Now, please," she demanded, her voice a breathy, erotic whisper in the silence of the room, and yanked at the ties. He reached down to tear them loose, freeing his cock. It slapped against her stomach, hot and hard, leaving a wet smear of pre-cum.

"Are you sure?" he stopped to look down at her even as he altered his position to fit the broad head against the entrance to her pussy. Desire gripped her and she nodded. He was big, but not big enough she couldn't take him.

"Please. Now, I need you..." She turned her head

to kiss the inside of his wrist where he was braced over her. "Now."

His answer was to push into her, parting her enough to slide in half an inch. She sucked a breath in as a burning sensation sliced through her, followed by pleasure. It hurt, but it was a good pain, one replaced with beautiful sensation.

"Harder." She gave voice to what they both wanted. He pushed again, and again, sliding deeper into her depths. Each time he did, she gripped him, as though her body was unwilling to let him go even to pull out of her long enough to slide back in.

"Fuck, you're tight." He collapsed onto his elbows over her, not crushing her but gathering her leg up over his hip. She helped by lifting the other and locking her ankles behind him. The change in position slid him deeper. They both groaned. "How can you be this tight? How can you...I..."

She blinked as he cut himself off, sure he'd been about to say something else, but he fell silent. His features tightened as he pulled back and powered into her again. Hard and fast, his rhythm set the couch beneath them to rocking as he took her, both still nearly fully dressed.

It was a wild ride, leaving her no options but to cling to him. He used every muscle in his body to taking her, bringing her pleasure until she was sure she couldn't take any more.

He'd been holding out, and at the end of the next stroke, rocked his hips. His pelvis pressed to hers, trapping her clit between them and she cried out. It felt so good... mind-numbingly, gotta-have-more kind of good.

"That," she panted. "Again."

He did, adding a roll at the end of every thrust, sending her need and arousal higher. Not for long though, within a few thrusts she teetered on the edge of the abyss, tendrils of pleasure reaching up to pull her into the depths.

"Come for me," he growled, slamming into her hard. "I want to hear you scream your pleasure. Want everyone to hear and know you're mine."

His. She was his.

With a cry, she gave in and screamed her pleasure for her alien lord.

HOURS LATER TARRICK WOKE, wrapped around his little human. She murmured in her sleep and made herself more comfortable on his bare chest. They'd moved during the night to the bed. Mindful that she wasn't as hardy as he was, he pulled the covers up around her to keep her warm.

He laid back, contentment washing over him. Humans. They'd been a total surprise. Tenacious, resourceful, and brave. Like smaller versions of the Lathar. Perhaps he should get Laarn to run tests to see if they were genetically related.

"Tarrick? You awake, you lazy ass?"

Speak of the devil and he will appear. Tarrick smiled as he reached over to tap the comms unit and froze. His gaze riveted to the inside of his wrist. Black marks on the skin wrapped around his wrist like creeper vines.

Familiar marks.

Marks that shouldn't be possible.

Couldn't be possible.

Eyes wide, he hit the comms button and brought his wrist closer.

"I'm awake, but we have a problem."

Laarn snorted. *"Tell me about it. The humans? They're—"*

"Genetically compatible," Tarrick finished for him. "I know."

"How the hell did you know that? The tests just came back."

Tarrick smiled and reached for his little human.

This would change the face of his world, of Lathar culture, but he didn't care.

"I know because I'm looking at a set of mating marks on my wrist."

His little human was his destined mate, and he would never let her go.

Ever.

9

*A*liens were as weird as humanity. Just when Cat thought she'd gotten the Latharian warriors worked out, they went and surprised her.

She lay on a diagnostic bed in the Healer's bay aboard the Velu'vias, the flagship captained by Tarrick K'Vass, War Commander of the Latharian Empire and all-round badass. *Her* badass, sexy alien warrior.

He'd claimed her as his when he and his men had captured Earth's frontier base, Sentinel Five, where she'd been stationed. She'd forgiven him for that, mostly. There were worse things than being the woman of a high-ranking alien hottie. There were also... advantages.

Like being able to help form policy on how the

Lathar dealt with their human captives, now that they'd realized humans weren't like any other species they'd enslaved. For one, they fought back, even when captured. Hunger strikes and passive resistance had confused Tarrick and his men. However, that was nothing compared to the escape and guerrilla warfare battle when a second, nastier group of aliens decided to steal the women Tarrick's group had captured.

They'd quickly found out that pissed-off human women with military training were more trouble than they were worth. *Way* more trouble. Right now, enemy warriors who survived the combined K'Vass attack/human resistance were cooling their heels in Tarrick's holding cells. They were currently leaderless and broken after Tarrick killed their leader for daring to lay a hand on Cat.

It had been more than a hand, but she shoved the unpleasant memories aside to focus on the here and now. She'd woken this morning to find Tarrick sitting by the bed, fully clothed, rather than naked and in it with her. Instantly, she'd known from his expression something was wrong. Rather than answer her, he'd made her dress and brought them both here.

She watched the holo-field arc over her body

shift and change. Latharian technology was massively more advanced than humanity's, but the holo-scanner reminded her of an MRI machine, even if it did seem to do...well, just about everything.

The symbols over her head moved down her body and she glanced at Tarrick on another scanner bed next to her. Because of the size difference between their species, she lay in the middle of the bed, but Tarrick, with his massive shoulders and hard, warrior's physique, dwarfed his.

Laarn, the lead healer aboard the ship, and as she'd learned Tarrick's twin brother, moved between the beds, studying both fields intensely. Like Tarrick and every other Lathar warrior she'd seen, he was tall and heavily muscled. That he was a doctor, as well, surprised her. Wearing the same leather uniform as the rest, although with a teal sash across his wide chest, he was more ready to go to war than into surgery.

He grunted at whatever the symbols said on the arc above her and turned to Tarrick. The field above her snapped off and she sat up to watch. Tarrick was stripped to the waist and she spent a pleasurable moment checking out her alien's ripped body. Where the hell had she gotten so lucky? Tarrick had the kind of build she'd only seen on holo-actors and porn-vid stars, and he was all hers to touch, and explore, and lick...

Snapping herself back to reality, she noticed Laarn focused his study on Tarrick's wrist. Black marks covered the skin, wrapping around his wrist a couple of times. They appeared odd, almost organic, as though vines were buried under the surface.

"What's that? Did you get a tattoo?" she asked, scooting to the edge of the bed. The designs hadn't been there last night. She slept like the dead though, so perhaps he'd nipped out to get it done while she'd been asleep.

Both men turned to her, identical frowns on their faces. Even if she hadn't known they were related, that expression right there would have clued her in.

"A tat-Oo?" Laarn asked, mangling the word. "What's that?"

Cat blinked as surprise rolled through her and thought back. She hadn't seen ink on any of the Lathar.

"Uhm, it's a body modification common among humans. Ink driven under the top layer of skin with needles to create a pattern or design." She leaned closer. The skin around the marks was red and raised, just like a new tattoo. "The skin heals to leave the design permanently in place."

"Needles? And humans do that voluntarily?" Tarrick wrinkled his nose in disgust. "How barbaric."

She chuckled. "Humans have some weird kinks. Tattoos are tame compared to some of the stuff out there."

Laarn studied her with an intent gaze, as though she'd just revealed something fascinating. Being the center of his attention was a little unsettling. Unlike Tarrick, no emotion softened his expression. It was like being studied under a microscope. "Do you have any?"

She shook her head. "Nope. But many people on the base have them if you wanted to take a closer look. My friend Jess has a large design on her back."

"Jess?" The big healer tapped out an enquiry on the console at the other side of Tarrick's bed.

"Jessica Kallson. She's a traffic control officer, like I am." A growl rumbled in Tarrick's throat. She sighed. "Okay, fine. Like I *was*."

"This her?" Laarn turned the screen to reveal an image of a young woman.

Cat nodded. "Yes. That's Jess. She was on the

flight deck the same time as I was. I haven't seen her since."

Guilt washed over her. She'd asked Tarrick to make sure her friend was okay, but hadn't seen her since the attack a few days ago.

"She's in stateroom three. One of the quiet ones, doesn't seem to be causing any trouble..." Laarn paused to read. "The preliminary medical scan came back okay. She's in good health and sustained no injuries in the attack."

Although she knew from Tarrick that Jess was okay, hearing the healer confirm it made her sigh in relief.

"I'll bring her in though, do a full check?" Laarn glanced over his shoulder, eyebrow arched.

"Thank you." She smiled her thanks. He seemed to have accepted her relationship with his brother without a qualm, and the fact that the link was important enough for him to check on her friend made her feel all kinds of warm and fuzzy inside. "So... if you guys don't have tattoos, what is that?"

They exchanged looks, and once again, she got the feeling there was more going on than they were admitting. Worry hit her, making her stomach churn and she slid off the bed to stand next to Tarrick. He kept trying to sit up, but Laarn reached out and shoved him down, none too gently.

After the third time, Tarrick blew out a breath. "You're enjoying this, aren't you? He rarely gets to shove me around anymore," he commented to Cat.

"Yeah, right. Just every time we spar. For a war commander, you're like a lumbering *Karatan.*" Laarn snorted, his green eyes sparkling with humor. "What my baby brother isn't telling you is that if I hadn't taken my healer's sash, I'd be the one running the ship, not him."

"Really? Is that how it works with you guys?" She smiled encouragingly, hoping they'd keep talking. Although they were over the first hurdle and the Lathar warriors were considering human women as more than mere possessions, the more she knew about their culture the better. No unpleasant surprises that way.

This time Tarrick spoke, laying still as Laarn scanned his wrist. "It's based on skill and ability. Laarn and I have been training since we could walk and because we're *Litaan* as well as siblings—"

"*Litaan?* That's your word for twins?"

He nodded. "Same height, same build, same abilities. It's down to performance on the day. And it *doesn't* mean Laarn would be running the ship. He decided to welch on facing me and wimped out to take his healer's trials."

"Trials? What...like exams?"

Laarn frowned, leaning forward to study the symbols on the holo-field as he answered. "Physical ones, yes."

"Ahh, yes. Our medical students have to do similar exams before they qualify. Simulations of operations and procedures, right?"

Laarn's hair danced on his leather-covered shoulders as he shook his head. His voice was flat and unemotional without the snarky tone she was used to hearing. "Not quite, no. All healers must experience every ailment and injury. The pain, the sensation, everything. Depending on how much they can handle...that will be the level of healer they become, then they're trained to that level."

"What?" Her jaw dropped in surprise. "But... that's...They do...They hurt you? So you can become a healer? Fuck no, *that's* barbaric!"

Tarrick chuckled and motioned at the bed around him. "The trials are simulated. Fool the brain the injuries are real."

"Oh, I see." She went quiet, feeling a little foolish.

Of course, they wouldn't intentionally injure

their own people just to see what kind of doctors they'd make. Then Laarn lifted his head and she caught a glimpse of his unguarded expression before the mask slid back into place, and her heart lurched. Pain lurked in the back of his eyes and she knew at that moment the suffering he'd gone through to become a healer was beyond most people's understanding.

"But Laarn made it through." Tarrick's voice rang with pride. "He's not only a healer, but the highest qualified healer in the Empire. He *should* be Lord Healer and control the Healer's Hall, but he opted to travel for a quadrasec instead. He's an asshole."

"Better than being a dickhead warrior."

Cat sighed and shook her head as the brothers' conversation devolved into insults and name-calling. Men, the same no matter what galaxy, obviously.

"Okay, so these marks..." She drew their attention back to the matter at hand. "Just so you know, all base staff are routinely checked for STDs, so if he's got something nasty, it didn't come from me." She shrugged when they both looked at her in surprise. "Just putting it out there."

"No. Not that." Laarn frowned. "Your people get infections from sex? That's..."

"Barbaric?" she guessed. It seemed to be Laarn's favorite word when it came to humans.

"No. It's a simple genetic fix though. So simple even a child could do it."

She raised an eyebrow. "Speaking as one of the 'children' present, we have a saying. If it ain't broke, don't fix it. Our doctors don't mess at the genetic level in case they make things worse."

"Huh. Interesting." Finally, Laarn snapped off the holo-field over Tarrick and leaned against the empty bed behind him, folding his arms over his chest.

His expression was neutral. That special blank expression doctors got when they were about to say something awful. Another similarity with humans. Ironic. Humanity had spent so long being scared of the possibility of little green men. Who would have guessed the aliens would be so similar on so many levels?

"I have good news and bad news."

Uh-oh, here it came. Mentally, she braced herself. At the same time, she employed logic. Surely with their massively more advanced technology, the Lathar could fix most things, right?

"The good news is these are exactly what I thought." He pointed to the marks wrapped around

Tarrick's wrist. "Somehow, unbelievably, humans are genetically compatible with the Lathar. Not only that, but I think they might be an offshoot. I'd need to run tests at the Healer's Hall to be sure."

Her world lurched sideways and Cat gaped at the healer. "We're Lathar? Not human?"

His shoulder lifted in a shrug. "Honestly, I can't tell at the moment, but it's a good possibility. There are too many similarities to be naturally occurring. To be sure I need to run deep level genetic scans and check all the markers."

He flicked a glance down at her stomach. "A quicker way to tell would be if you'd already fallen pregnant, but I checked and you haven't."

Huh. She hadn't even considered a baby, not with what Tarrick told her about his species' reproduction problems. "That could happen?"

"Possibly, yes."

Shit.

"And the bad news?"

Laarn smiled. "They're mating marks, so you're stuck with my idiot brother. You're...what do you humans call it? Married."

～

TARRICK HATED WAITING. For anything. He particularly hated waiting on the Emperor while stuck in a non-combat bot. Actually, he just hated the non-combat bots. A little under his natural height, with none of the on-board weaponry or improvements of his own custom-built combat machine, it was restrictive and cramped.

Worse yet, he was surrounded by courtiers as they all waited for the Emperor to emerge from his bed-chamber. They reclined on low padded couches, talking in soft voices. Tarrick used the machine's central eye to study them without them being aware, not that they'd bothered much with the bot anyway. He'd deliberately picked up a standard palace model rather than one which would show his family affiliation and rank, so their sycophantic tendencies hadn't been triggered. If they knew who he was in the metal shell, they'd have been all over him like a bad rash. The sister-son of the Emperor, he was considered part of the Imperial family. One reason he preferred to be incognito here.

Tarrick sighed, his bot body clicking as it inflated its mechanical chest in an approximation of the movement. Most wouldn't have been able to trigger the machine to make the movement, but Tarrick was an extremely experienced pilot. His control of the neural connection needed to operate the avatars was an almost perfect mesh of the biological and technological.

He'd even qualified on the bigger *Drakeen* bots. Heavily armed and armored, they could take on hordes of combat bots by themselves, but were hellishly difficult to pilot. There were only a handful of *Drakeen*-qualified pilots across the entire empire. He was one, as was the Emperor.

The chatter in the room stopped when the big double doors to the Emperor's bed-chamber opened. His Imperial Majesty Daaynal K'Saan strode into the room, resplendent in his warrior's leathers complete with his imperial sash—a dark, regal purple—across his chest. He was a born emperor, rather than one who had gained his position through conquest, so his sash was single color and unadorned. Warrior's braids peeked through the mass of black hair that cascaded over his shoulders.

Tarrick straightened, catching the Emperor's eye as he strode past courtiers scrambling to free themselves from the low couches. Daaynal stopped, looked Tarrick's bot up and down, then snapped an order over his shoulder. "Leave us."

There was a mass exodus. Courtiers raced to be

the first to do the Emperor's bidding, resulting in a pile up by the door. The servos in the bot's neck whirred as he watched the stampede. "I have no idea why you put up with them, your majesty."

The last courtier got his cloak stuck in the door trying to get through. Frantically trying to free the heavily tasseled and ornate garment, he glanced up, realized they were both watching him and squeaked. A yank and the sound of tearing fabric later, he disappeared through the door like a *gethal* down its burrow.

Daaynal's lips quirked. "Entertainment value?"

He turned back to Tarrick and grabbed the bot by its metallic shoulders, looking at the avatar with fond affection, as though Tarrick were there in the flesh. "So, my sister-son, tell me how things have developed with your humans?"

The words, and the warm tone of voice they were uttered in warmed Tarrick's heart. Twins didn't run in the K'Vass family. Rather, they ran in the imperial line. His mother, Miisan, had been Daaynal's *Litaan,* his twin. Every time he looked at his uncle, he saw his mother's eyes. That Daaynal insisted on preserving the special relationship that existed between a man and his nephew's past childhood was something neither Tarrick nor Laarn had expected.

"Things go well, which is the reason I'm here to speak to you." He turned as Daaynal looped a massive arm over 'his' shoulders and turned toward the large windows at the end of the chamber. "They are technologically inferior, but in attitude and ferocity, they easily match us."

"Really?" Daaynal's eyebrow winged up as he leaned one massive shoulder against the window frame and gazed out on the gardens below. The Herris blossom, the symbol of the Imperial family, was in full bloom. The sight of them, his mother's favorite flower, never failed to ease Tarrick's heart. "The males are much smaller than us though, correct?"

Tarrick didn't bother to hide his smile. Daaynal couldn't see it on the unemotional face of the bot, but he wouldn't have hidden his amusement anyway.

"They are, but I wasn't talking about the males."

Confusion flittered over Daaynal's face for a second before a sound by the door made them turn. An Oonat, graceful in her hooded robes, slipped from the Emperor's bed-chamber. No prizes for guessing why. Daaynal needed an heir, even an oonat-born one.

Latharian DNA was dominant, so no child born

of such a union would be a half-breed. Such children were always male, completely Lathar. His cousin Fenriis, for example, was oonat-born, and he was more Lathar in his upbringing and mannerisms than either Tarrick or his brother.

And no one was more eager for Daaynal to beget an heir than Tarrick. His brother wouldn't be able to avoid the Lord Healer's position for much longer, and his calling there surpassed even that of the imperial throne. Which meant Tarrick himself was next in line. That didn't mean it would be all plain sailing though. Because his claim was through a maternal line, there were at least four other warriors with claims they'd fight to the death for. He'd avoid a power struggle for the throne. He was happy being a War Commander, with his lovely little Cat by his side. Although...she *would* make a beautiful empress.

"Then who were you speaking about?"

"The females. It seems humans don't have the same issues we do with numbers. Their gender numbers are equal. So much so, the base we attacked had female military personnel."

Daaynal stilled, his focus solely on Tarrick. "They don't protect their women? What kind of species are they? Like the Oonat?"

Tarrick laughed. "*Draanth,* no. They mounted a robust defense to our attack on their base but eventually lost to superior technology. Not for want of trying though. We secured their base and separated the males from the females as usual. That's when we ran into problems. These females are not civilians. They're as highly trained in weapons and tactics as the men. We couldn't get any information out of them on questioning, and they were offering passive resistance until the T'Laat arrived."

The Emperor's expression tightened for a second before his face cleared. It didn't last more than a blink of the eye, but Tarrick spotted the brief flare of dislike and anger. Daaynal didn't like the T'Laat, everyone knew that, but as emperor, he couldn't play favorites.

"And then?" he asked.

"The T'Laat made the mistake of kidnapping the women."

"I'm assuming since you're talking to me now and you're only just mentioning it, that you have the situation sorted? How many women did you lose?" Daaynal grimaced and reached a hand up to run through his long hair. "Fuck, I didn't want the T'Laat in that sector. Now they know there are women there. They'll be impossible to get rid—"

"None," Tarrick interrupted, "We didn't lose any women. They'd already figured out our ident tags were the key to accessing ship systems. They stole one from Varish, used it to open a weapons cache. By the time we boarded the ship with combat teams, they'd freed themselves, bottlenecked the T'Laat forces and were blowing the *draanth* out of them."

This time Daaynal's eyes did widen in surprise. Then he laughed. "By the ancestors, they sound perfect. Almost as bad as we are."

"Yeah, that. You might want to take a look at this." Using the same subspace link he used to control the bot, Tarrick quickly sent the images of his wrist and medical data Laarn supplied, showing them on the chest-mounted screen on the bot.

"Fuck me..." If he'd ever wanted to see Daaynal surprised, he was seeing it now. The bigger man's expression was one of utter shock. "If there is even the *chance* they are what Laarn thinks, I want to see. I want to meet some. Bring them here."

10

"*T*he Emperor wants to see us? Really?"

Cat followed in Tarrick's wake like a little lost puppy following its master. The impression wasn't helped by the fact she had to trot to keep up. Every long stride of his needed at least two of hers, maybe even three. It was demeaning, but at the moment she didn't care. She was more interested in what he had to say than any blow to her pride.

"He does. He was most interested when I told him about your species and in particular this." He twisted his wrist in a telling gesture. The marks were covered by the long sleeves of his jacket, and a wrist bracer for good measure.

She appreciated the foresight. If every Latharian warrior realized that, unlike the oonat, humans could trigger their long-dormant mating marks, it would be open season. Competition for a human woman, any human woman, could cause chaos and dissent in the ranks, potentially shattering war clans.

The soldier in her wanted to insist that wouldn't be a bad thing. A fractured enemy was easier to combat, but she had to be sensible about this. Under the control of a sympathetic war commander, the Lathar could negotiate with humanity, sign treaties, and build alliances. But scattered lone-wolf groups of warriors would just invade and take what they wanted when they wanted, and humanity could do little about it. And not all Lathar were as honorable as the K'Vass.

Cat shuddered, remembering Varish T'Laat. The last thing any human woman needed was to be at the mercy of such a monster. No, the best way forward was to put their lot in with the K'Vass and hope the Latharian emperor was as "easy" to deal with.

Besides, she'd always wanted to see new planets and civilizations. It had been the main reason she'd signed up for the Sentinel program; to explore, to be out there on the frontier in a way humanity never had been before. So the chance to see the Lathar homeworld was an opportunity the explorer in her couldn't pass up.

"What's he like?" she asked as they entered the flight bay. She'd gotten used to the fact everything to do with the Lathar was just, well, bigger. Their ship, their furniture, their clothing...their men. Hell, were their men build bigger. *All* over. She dragged her mind away from the gutter quickly and looked around. After a while, she'd gotten used to the larger proportions. It took something like the flight deck— easily big enough to fit a couple of terran destroyers in—to make her appreciate the size difference.

They strode past row on row of fighters. Like the combat avatars present as guards throughout the ship and the main force which attacked her base, they were remote controlled. The pilots' lounge was one place Tarrick refused to allow her. Said something about human women were dangerous enough with the knowledge they'd gathered already; he wasn't handing over any more of the Lathar's secrets on a plate. She'd smirked at that. From assuming humans were simple and easily cowed, the Lathar learnt they might be smaller, but a force to be reckoned with. Especially when they got hold of energy weapons.

"Daaynal? He's a K'Saan. Think Laarn but bigger, same eyes."

She hurried to pull even with him, reaching out a hand to his arm as they turned a corner. A quick glance took in the small group waiting at the end of the row, but she ignored them in favor of curiosity, looking at Tarrick.

"Same eyes? Why would he have the same eyes as your brother?"

Tarrick gave her a sexy little side-glance through the corner of his eye. "Because Laarn has our mother's eyes, and Daaynal was our mother's *Litaan.*"

She paused, her steps faltering as the words sunk in. Holy crap...

"You mean you're a prince? You're a freaking alien prince and you never told me?" She ran to catch up, swinging around to stand in front of him, her tone accusing. "Why didn't you say you were royalty?"

He stopped finally and looked down at her, his golden eyes narrowed. "Would it have made any difference to how you viewed me? That some accident of my birth was more important than the skills and status I have gained on my own?"

Shit. Put like that it sounded bad. "No, of course not. But your culture fascinates me... probably fascinates all of us. Like your clans, your names...the relationships between you."

She'd quickly come to realize the Lathar in a war clan were usually related in some way. Cousins at least. None seemed to be as closely related as Tarrick and Laarn though.

He sighed, but she caught the softer expression in his eyes before it disappeared. It pleased him, her interest in his family. "Yes, I'm technically what your people would call a prince, as is Laarn. And although Karryl shares our father's blood, he is a J'Vass. The clan only gained the right to use the K' signifier when my mother took my father as bond-mate. The K' indicates a line descended from Imperial blood."

She nodded, soaking up as much information as she could while they walked. She'd thought the different names were, while pretty, just that. She hadn't realized they meant something. "Karryl is related to you as well?"

He nodded. "The son of my father's younger brother."

They'd almost reached the small group waiting for them near a docked ship larger than most of the flyers on the deck. If Cat had to guess, she'd put it about the same size as the Captain's Yacht on the base. A fast, luxury transporter for a few VIP passengers. Only this wasn't built like any luxury carrier she'd ever seen. It had far too much armor and weaponry. But then again, that was in line with everything about the Lathar. Their whole culture was based on warfare.

The group contained tall, leather-clad warriors and a small group of women dressed much like she was, in long robes and warm capes. Oddly, for an advanced culture, Latharian fashion tended toward the medieval. Along with the clothing change from their dirty uniforms, she'd noticed a distinct thawing in the attitude of the women to their Latharian "captors."

Her gaze flicked over the women, then shot back to one familiar figure.

"Jess!" she squealed, launching herself across the space between them to hug her friend.

Okay, so it was a bear hug around the neck and caused the taller woman to stagger back a bit but Cat didn't care. She just hugged her friend harder.

"Might want to let her breathe a little?" Laarn, behind them, pointed out.

"Yeah...breathing would be good," Jess gasped, although her hold on Cat was just as tight.

Reluctantly, she eased her grip and studied her

friend. Apart from the tiredness around her eyes, Jess appeared in good health.

"I'm so glad you're here. Things have been..." She paused, words drying up as she tried to verbalize the events of the last few days. Jess smiled and grabbed her hands to squeeze them. "I know, don't worry, I know. Just...I'm here, you're here. Let's work from that, eh?"

"Yeah..." Cat's breath shuddered from her lungs and she looked up to find Laarn watching them. His gaze was locked onto Jess, his expression possessive until he noticed her watching him. Instantly his face blanked and he gave her a smooth smile. So, the aloof healer did have a weakness after all. She smiled at him, mouthing "*thank you*," sure Laarn was the reason Jess had been included on this trip.

He didn't reply, looking away without acknowledging her thanks. She didn't argue because a commotion behind them caught their attention. The group turned to find Jane Allen stalking toward them with Karryl dogging her steps.

"You were injured, female. You should be resting, not running around the ship risking further injury." Frustration obvious in his voice, the big warrior danced around Jane, trying to get her to stop so he could lift her in his arms. His strange half-scuttle and scoop with his arms spread wide made Cat chuckle, a sound she quickly smothered as the soap opera in front of them unfolded.

"I'm all right," Jane hissed, her gaze focused on the group by the transport as though Karryl were nothing to do with her. "How am I going to come to harm on a ship this well armed?"

Somehow, she'd managed to avoid the robes and cape combo the rest of them had and wore leather pants a la Latharian warrior and a singlet vest. Her dog tags bounced against her chest as she walked. She'd even managed to keep her boots, which somehow fit with her mishmash ensemble. All in all, the Marine looked badass. A fact that didn't escape the attention of the two other warriors with the group, who sucked quick breaths in at the sight of the human woman.

She, however, wasn't paying any attention to their little group, mainly because at that moment Karryl had decided enough was enough and tried to scoop her up over his shoulder. The women, knowing what was coming, winced.

He'd no sooner got his hands around Jane's trim waist when she turned the tables on him. Grabbing his arm, she twisted and turned in a quick movement that dumped the big warrior on the floor.

To add insult to injury, she dropped and pinned one arm with a knee, jamming her other booted foot right in his throat.

"Don't you ever try that again, sunshine," she warned, her voice cold and level. "You lot might have all these young women atwitter with the muscles and the charm... But I'm older, wiser and with a shitload more experience under my belt of dealing with pretty boy soldiers like you."

Cat leaned in to whisper in Tarrick's ear. "She likes him."

His eyes widened. "She does? How can you tell?"

She hid her smile. "She hasn't killed him yet."

Jane rolled away, and Karryl scrambled to his feet. Glaring around, he spotted Laarn. "Healer, do something about this defective female! Make her understand what an honor it is to be chosen by a warrior of my standing."

Jane snorted, boot stomping on the deck she joined them. "Stow it, big boy. Humans don't consider it an 'honor' when a guy wants to stick his dick in her. You've got a hand, I suggest you put it to use if that's all you're interested in."

The women dissolved into giggles quickly smothered when Karryl glared at them.

Tarrick sighed. "Children! If you're finished, the Emperor awaits."

As Cat expected, the yacht was utilitarian, set up more for combat than luxury. The metal of the bulkheads in the corridors they passed was unadorned, and at no point on their journey through the ship did she see carpeting covering the deck plates. The design was simple, with barracks and other rooms off the central corridor. At one end was the "bridge," little more than a fancy cockpit, and at the other was a large common room.

All the rooms had their own facilities, though, for which she was thankful. She didn't fancy wandering the central corridor at night trying to find a toilet. Not that she thought any of the warriors aboard would even look at her sideways, but a girl liked her privacy, especially when bed head was an option.

Voices rose in the corridor behind them as Laarn assigned rooms. None of the warriors were bunked with a human woman, a fact Karryl argued intensely about. From what Cat could gather, Karryl thought his claim over Jane was a done deal, and her consent a mere formality. Meanwhile, Jane was simply ignoring the big warrior. Tarrick led Cat up a flight of stairs tucked in a corner. Cat hid her smirk and followed Tarrick.

The flight of stairs led to a secondary deck. Smaller than the main one, it was one room, with a large bed set in the middle of the wall under a sloping picture window. Clearly designed so the occupant could gaze at the stars. There were two doors in the wall opposite. She raised her eyebrow at Tarrick in question.

"Washroom and storage," he replied quickly. Absently.

His attention was all on her, steady gold gaze unwavering. It was impossible to look away, and her heart rate increased as the gold became darker, more heated.

She knew that expression. Her body knew it well.

"Tarrick, we don't have time."

"Nonsense. There's plenty of time... Or did you forget, I give the orders around here."

She backed as he stalked her, somehow managing to get himself between the door to the stairs and her. Not that it mattered, if she ran it wouldn't be very far. He'd catch her in the corridor below, where she knew he'd take her anyway, regardless of whom watched.

"Around here... Yes. But have you forgotten about the Emperor?"

He shrugged and continued to stalk her. "Laarn will get us underway."

There was no arguing with that, so she didn't bother, her lips curving into a smile as he reached her. Snagging a hand around her waist, he pulled her against his hard, muscled body and claimed her lips.

She melted, her knees weak as he swept his tongue past her lips to plunder her mouth. His tongue found hers, sliding against it in sensual strokes that took her breath away. The small whimper in the back of her throat was purely instinctive and she drove her hands into his short hair to hold him to her.

His kiss turned hard, frenzied, and she broke away to gasp. That didn't stop him, his lips blazing a trail down the length of her throat. Held in his iron embrace, she couldn't escape. Didn't want to escape. Ever.

Strong fingers shoved the cape from her shoulders, the fabric pooling at her feet. She shivered as the cooler air of the room hit her bare shoulders. The dichotomy of the chill and the heat from his body drove her crazy. She moved closer, her hips urgent against his as the fever in her blood grew. Need became all encompassing and she tore at the zipper at the front of his uniform. Anything to get to the smooth, silken skin over his hard, muscled chest. A chest and a body she would never tire of exploring.

"Fuck...you're hot. So sexy," he muttered and claimed her lips with open-mouthed, hard kisses. His hands tangled in the straps of her dress, yanking them down with a twist that unraveled the alien design of the garment. It slithered down her body, leaving her naked apart from the heeled sandals he'd had her wear this morning.

He gripped her shoulders, putting some space between them. His eyes burned with passion. He didn't speak. Instead, his face tightened, hardened until his features became almost cruel.

She squeaked as he spun her around with a quick movement and pushed her toward the bed. The push and the unaccustomed heels made her stumble, and she half fell across the soft surface. As she got to her knees, he wrapped his sash around her wrists with a lightning fast movement. Securing them to the bedpost at the foot of the bed, he pulled the fabric tight until she bent at the waist. Hard fingers dug into the sides of her hips, pulling her ass up even as a large, booted foot kicked her feet apart.

"Tarrick! Slow down!" Her exclamation devolved into a small moan when he swept a finger through her already wet folds. Shit, that felt too good.

"As you pointed out, the Emperor is waiting," he rumbled, rough voice carrying a trace of amusement as she lifted her ass for more of his attentions. Bastard. He knew he only had to touch her for her to go up in flames. "So, this'll have to be quick."

The broad tip of his finger collected the slick juice of her arousal and rubbed it over her clit. She whimpered, biting her lower lip to stop from crying out as he worked her body. Rubbed over and around the little nubbin of flesh, then, when she was least expecting it, gave her a little spank. There. Right there. On her clit.

"Yeoooohhh!" she moaned, the soft tap intensifying her pleasure in a way she hadn't expected. No time to reflect though, because he started to rub again. Teasing and caressing her clit, adding the short little taps that didn't hurt, exactly, but soon had her arching back against him. She needed him to fill her... cock, fingers, anything. Just now. Sooner.

He didn't. Instead, he drove her to the edges of her endurance, rubbing and teasing until her hips rocked and the moans that rolled from her lips merged into one soft sound of need. It didn't take long, her orgasm rushing up faster than it ever had and then she was there, balanced on the precipice.

And he moved his hands.

"No!" She couldn't help the moan that escaped her. So close. She needed him to touch her, stroke more. Take her over the edge and into the rolling abyss of pleasure that awaited when she fell.

He grunted, moving behind her, and then her attention was all on the broad head of his cock where it pressed against her. Not for long. Adjusting himself, he pushed his long, thick length into her in a single, hard stroke.

"Fuck!" she gasped, fingers curled into claws with pleasure. He was big, so big, but she loved the feeling of being stretched. The throb of her pussy around his cock. The friction the tight fit afforded. Even the burning pleasure-pain when he first entered her.

"That was the idea. Or did you have something else in mind?" As he spoke, he pulled back and thrust again, drawing out the tight, burning ecstasy of his initial penetration. She was back to biting her lip, trying to contain her sounds of pleasure.

With her bent over in front of him, he set up a hard and fast pace, slamming into her over and over. She couldn't move, but she didn't care. Her body was a mass of hypersensitive nerve endings all attuned to his every movement. Tightness coiled within her, drawing into a tight knot in her core.

Reaching around her, one large hand covered her left breast, tweaking and pinching the nipple. A line of fire arrowed down to her clit, making it throb, as though it and her nipple were connected. She panted, shoving her ass back against him with each thrust. That was it. Wouldn't take her much longer. Just a little more.

He reached around with the other hand, sliding it between her thighs and tweaked her clit.

It was all she needed.

She shattered, screaming his name as she came.

11

When Cat and Tarrick rejoined the rest aboard the vessel, they were well underway and everyone was gathered in the common area at the back of the ship. All eyes turned toward them as the door opened, and Cat ducked her head, cheeks flaming at the knowing looks the women shot them. The warriors were either clueless or far too worried about Tarrick's reaction to bat an eyelid.

They wore leather uniforms, but with the jackets unzipped to show their hard, sculptured chests. When they'd left their quarters, she'd thought Tarrick was just lazy. Now though, she realized it was more than that. The half-undressed deal seemed to be more akin to casual dress for them.

"Ey, ey...the lovebirds return," Kenna smirked as Cat slid into the seat next to Jess, which earned her a play cuff around the ear from Jane behind her. She ducked, laughed, and stuck her tongue in her cheek while hollowing the other in the universal gesture for a blowjob.

"There's always one." Cat sighed, shaking her head at the woman's antics and took the glass Jess held out to her. "What's this?"

"Tastes like lemonade," Jane answered, lifting her glass in salute. "Just be careful and go slow. It's got quite the kick, as you can see." She nodded toward Kenna, who bristled with indignation. "I am not drunk!"

Her denial fell on deaf ears because right at that moment Laarn chose to remove his jacket. Instantly he had the attention of every woman in the room. Like Tarrick, he was tall, broad-shouldered and heavily-muscled. Unlike Tarrick, he had shoulder length dark hair that brushed his shoulders.

And scars.

Everywhere.

They crisscrossed his pecs and over his arms. Fine scars like lace over his skin, old and faded, but that still looked painful. Farther down, deeper marks highlighted his rib cage, also healed and old. A single, thick scar ran down the center of his chest, reminiscent of old style open-heart surgery back on earth. It trailed down, disappearing under the low cut pants.

"Fucking *hell*..." Kenna murmured what they were all thinking. How much had he suffered? And why?

Unable to tear her eyes away as Laarn folded his jacket and turned to a kitchenette in the corner of the room, Cat leaned toward Tarrick, seated next to her. "What happened to him?"

Tarrick leaned against the padded back of the seat, arm spread behind her. "All healers have them. From their trials."

She looked at him, not bothering to hide her shock. "I thought you said it was holo-stuff... simulation? That he wasn't actually hurt?"

"No, he wasn't. But the injuries were real to the mind, which caused a reaction in the body." Tarrick's expression was neutral. "It's why we never use lifelike avatars. It's the same technology. If we used something that felt too right, too similar to our real bodies and the machine 'dies' we'd die too."

The shudder rolled from her toes, raced up her spine, and crawled over her scalp. "So becoming a healer could have killed him?"

Tarrick's expression was blank and polite, but Cat was quickly coming to realize the Lathar put up a mask when they wanted to hide something, much like humans. She stayed silent and kept eye contact, a trick she'd learned years before. Most people felt uncomfortable and automatically filled the silence. A quick flare of lighter gold in his eyes told her that he knew what she was doing, but finally he gave a small nod of his head.

Not to be outdone by Laarn, Karryl started to strip his own jacket. Like the rest of the Lathar, he was tall and heavily muscled but...bigger. He made Laarn and Tarrick seem like greyhounds in comparison. Kenna, well through her glass of the alien lemonade, wolf-whistled in approval as the warrior strutted his stuff, eyes on Jane.

"See, female? Your companions find me appealing," he said, puffing his chest out.

Kenna muttered something, catching an elbow from Jess for it and toppled over backward off the bench.

Jane shook her head. "She's drunk. She'd find anything with a dick appealing."

"Hey!" Kenna complained from the floor. "I resemble that remark!"

"Karryl, if you're finished trying to show off?"

Laarn's voice cut through the banter like a heated knife through butter. "I'm trying to show the women what food they're likely to be offered at the Emperor's court."

At the word *food*, the women in the room were all ears, even Cat. So far she'd eaten what Tarrick ate, which was some field ration slop that tasted a bit like porridge. After a couple of days on the stuff, she'd kill for something with a little more flavor and texture.

"Okay, these are all typical dishes at court," Laarn said as he started to place bowls on the counter between them. He moved quickly, with a quiet efficiency that was mesmerizing. With a quick glance up, he offered a small smile. "Come on, they won't bite."

Chairs scraped, glasses forgotten in the stampede for the counter. Even tipsy, Kenna managed to get herself off the floor and fought for a place near the food. The kitchenette counter was small, with a hot plate on one side and the bowls on the other. Laarn had put a pot on the hot plate and poured something gloopy and brown into it to heat before he turned back to them.

"This is *kervaas*." He pointed to the first bowl. The contents were gray, slimy, and wriggling.

"Ugh. Worms?" Jess wrinkled her nose in disgust.

"If that's what you call them." Laarn shrugged. "They grow on certain grasses and are highly nutritious. Gather enough and it'll keep a warrior going for a day."

"What's this?" Cat leaned forward to peer into the next bowl. It contained what looked like flat strips of dried meat, like jerky.

"*Veritan,*" Tarrick answered for him, reaching over to snag a piece. He turned Cat toward him, offering it to her lips. "Try it, it's good."

She smiled and took a little bite. The taste of spice and sweetness exploded onto her tongue and she groaned. "Oh my god, that is *so* good. Guys, you have to try some of this."

The rest dived in, plucking strips of the meat from the bowl. Moans of appreciation filled the room. Laarn looked up and grinned at Karryl. "See, warrior? I can do with my cooking what you couldn't with all your posturing."

Karryl snarled, snapping something Cat couldn't pick up.

They went through several other bowls, with different forms of meat and some with salad and vegetables. Finally, Laarn set a plate on the table and reached for the pan he'd been heating. With careful movements, he ran a knife around the brown mass in the pan, then flipped it over and out onto the plate.

"Cake!"

"Oh my god, is that chocolate cake?"

"Laarn, I think I love you."

The healer grinned, actually grinned, as he cut the cake and handed each of the women a piece. Cat cradled hers carefully. It was still warm, but not too hot to eat. Tentatively she broke off a corner and popped it into her mouth.

Heaven melted onto her tongue. Hot, delicious, sweet heaven. It was like the best, expensive chocolate cake she'd ever tasted that faded into a mousse when she chewed.

"Blow me, that is *the* best chocolate cake I've ever had!" Once again Kenna was the one to say what they all felt, with moans of accompaniment from the rest of them. Halfway through the cake, though, the Marine paused, then wrinkled her nose.

"How fattening is this?" she demanded suddenly, her focus intent on Laarn who was cutting more cake. "You guys are not like feeding us up or something are you?"

Laarn paused, surprise washing over his

features. "Why would we want you as anything other than how you are?"

"I've seen it in the holos." Once on a topic, Kenna was difficult to dissuade. "Men who like bigger women. Feed them up and all that. Because I'll tell you something, I worked my *ass* off for an ass like this. Squats man, you have *no* idea how many squats. And I'm not having it all ruined because of your wicked chocolate cake."

Laarn looked confused.

"You mean will it make you gain weight? Highly unlikely, the active ingredient raises metabolism. It's why we don't cook it when operational. Our nutritional needs would go through the roof."

Cat blinked a couple of times as she mentally translated healer 'speak.' "You mean it's good chocolate cake? It makes you burn the calories you eat?"

Laarn tilted his head to the side as though he were working out her words. Then he nodded. "Yes. It will do that. Makes your body more efficient."

The women all gaped at him.

"Screw hot as hell aliens," Kenna said, taking another slice. "Man, you got every earth woman's dream right here... Chocolate cake that doesn't make you fat."

THEY HADN'T BEEN BACK to Lathar Prime, physically, for far too long.

Two days later, Tarrick and his warriors stood in the tiny airlock of the commander's transport. The human women were tucked into the middle of the crowded space as they waited for the door in front of them to cycle and open. There was far too much male in such an enclosed area. He could feel the same eagerness radiating from them that coiled within him.

The door clunked and he looked down at Cat standing next to him. A wash of pleasure and love rolled through him. He still couldn't believe how lucky he was. Couldn't believe he'd found the one woman in the galaxy who had been able to pull the mating marks to life within his skin. All he'd had to do was cross the galaxy and search a backwater system for her.

She smiled up at him, her eyes alight with intelligence and humor. With her traditional robes and cape, and her hair piled up to bare her slender neck, she looked so lovely, she took his breath away. Heat exploded through him like an energy blast and he had to fight the urge to drag her up to his cabin and have his way with her.

Again.

Before he could move though, the door clicked a final time and rolled open. His desire was overruled by his need to see how Cat reacted to his home planet. What would she think? Would she like it? Could she see herself living here?

"Oh my, it's beautiful." Hand raised to her lips, his little Cat moved forward to the edge of the airlock and peered out. She was quickly joined by the other women and Tarrick had to smile. They looked for all the worlds like *Deearin* kits about to escape their mother's den and venture into the world for the first time.

He hadn't let any of them see out any of the viewports as they'd landed. Instead, he'd kept the blast shields up so they'd get the full effect of seeing the Emperor's court for the first time. It appeared to have worked.

"It's like ancient Greece or something."

"Awesome columns. How high do you think they are?"

Tarrick half listened to the women's chatter as he signaled his men to move. Absently, he wondered if all earth women talked so much. It was enough to give any warrior a damn headache. A constant stream of verbal...noise. But despite the fact they didn't seem able to keep silent, he was very aware they were moving as a military unit.

The one they called Jane had taken point, her odd-eyed gaze sharp and assessing as she looked around. Of them all, she was the least talkative. Tarrick flicked a glance to Karryl, who was paying more attention to the lithe human than on his surroundings. Perhaps that was a blessing. Karryl, while he had a heart of *siivas,* was famous for his short-temper.

In the middle were his own Cat and her friend, Jess, flanked on the other side by his brother. At the back, with Gaarn and Talat behind her, was the sassy-mouthed Kenna. He glanced over his shoulder to see her half turn, her keen gaze scanning the rear. She caught him watching her when she turned back and winked at him. Plainly she knew he knew what she was doing and didn't care.

Shaking his head at the odd behavior of human women, he turned and concentrated on getting them to the court and to the Emperor. Like the rest of his warriors, he bristled with weaponry. Court dress for a Lathar consisted of attitude, armor, and as many weapons as a male could carry. Although elegant, the Emperor's palace was a dangerous place. All warriors were armed—regardless of rank or status¬—and challenges were common. Extremely common.

Which meant no one was surprised when their path was blocked by a small group of warriors. R'Zaa. Their facial features were distinct. The warrior at the front Tarrick recognized. J'aett, the son of the clan leader.

"I heard you'd found women," he commented, his gaze assessing the human women. They stood still, not an ounce of subservience in their manners as they glared back at him. Not one of them gasped or backed up, making him proud. They didn't behave like the weak species the Lathar had originally taken them for.

Still didn't stop him wanting to spread J'aett's nose all over his face. Especially when he gave Cat the once over. But it was Jane, at the front of the group with her arms folded and a "fuck you" expression that caught his attention the most. Unlike the rest, she wore a strange combination of lathar and terran clothing and her bearing marked her as exactly what she was: a soldier.

The R'Zaa warrior stepped forward, reaching out to grab Jane. "I claim this one."

Karryl moved faster than Tarrick had ever seen him move, shoving between J'aett and his prey to knock the other warrior's hand aside.

"Too late, *draanthic*," he snarled. "She's already claimed."

The other warriors closed ranks around the rest of the women, and Tarrick shot a look at Jane, shaking his head to warn her not to argue Karryl's claim over her. Not here. Not now. The R'Zaa had almost as bad a reputation as the T'Laat. No human woman wanted to find herself at their mercy, not as a slave.

He didn't want any human woman being claimed outside the K'Vass until he'd had a chance to petition the Emperor to have their status as a lost offshoot of the Lathar confirmed. Once that happened then all Lathar would have to honor them, and to injure one would be punishable by death. A death he'd be happy to mete out personally, he realized. Somewhere along the way he'd become protective of the humans.

"Yeah?" J'aett wasn't put off that easily. He backed up a few steps, the warriors behind him scattering, and motioned to Karryl. "Then I guess I'll have to challenge you for her. Unless you don't think you're up to it..."

Karryl snarled and launched himself forward, blade in hand, accepting the challenge through action rather than words. J'aett met him mid-attack, twin blades flashing in the air as battle was joined. Karryl was bigger, but J'aett was lighter and faster. Tarrick held his position, hand itching to go for his own blades as the two fought, dancing around each other, but held off. All Karryl needed was one blow, a knockout, and it would be over.

But it didn't look good, not with the R'Zaa warrior dancing rings around him. Jane tried to leap forward to help, only Laarn's arm around her waist stopping her. Her features were wreathed in worry and fear. Not for herself, but for the big warrior being cut to ribbons by his smaller opponent. Tarrick blanked his smile. So, despite her protests, the human did have feelings for his warrior.

"Please," Cat tugged on his arm. "Aren't you going to help him?"

Tarrick shook his head. "Challenge fight. If we intervene, Karryl will be pissed. It will be like us saying he can't handle it. That he's not man enough."

"He's bleeding!" she protested, her stubborn lips setting in a line. "How can you stand there and not help him?"

"Seriously, Moore Cat," he allowed her a small smile, "he can take it. Believe me."

J'aett leapt, spinning in the air to land a hard kick across Karryl's jaw and for a moment, Tarrick though that was it, the R'Zaa had actually gotten the better of the big warrior. Karryl grunted and fell to his knees.

"*NO!*" Jane bellowed, fighting Laarn's hold.

"You'll be mine, little one." J'aett took his eyes off the fallen warrior to leer at Jane.

Which was the moment Karryl made his move. Flicking his dark hair out of his eyes, he dropped to the floor and spun on his hands, twisting his body and scissoring his legs to tangle in J'aett's. The R'Zaa tumbled to the ground, Karryl over him in a heartbeat. Pinning J'aett's arms to the ground, he raised his fist. Before he could deliver the knockout blow though, one of J'aett's warriors pulled an energy pistol and aimed it at the side of Karryl's head. "Not so fast."

Tarrick and his men froze. This was not how challenge fights went. Karryl had won, all the rules stated as such, and for the R'Zaa to pull weapons was a clear violation of protocol. On an ordinary day, Tarrick and his men would happily take on the other clan, and anyone else who wanted to pile in, but now they had the women to protect... That changed things. He couldn't allow any of them to be hurt.

A flash of fabric fluttered in the corner of Tarrick's eye. Kenna stepped behind the R'Zaa warrior and pressed the muzzle of a pulse pistol firmly against the back of his skull.

Oh. Shit. Tarrick's eyes widened. This was not going to end well.

"I've never trained with these weapons, just on our type. At this range I figure it'll probably make a mess of whatever, if anything, you got in that pretty little head of yours." All traces of the joking woman Tarrick had seen before were gone. Her hand was unwavering and her voice cold as she spoke. "Now how about you let my friend's man go and I won't redecorate with your brains. How about that?"

Before anyone could react to Kenna's bold move, a cold voice cut through the tension.

"Would someone like to explain why this... woman is threatening to redecorate my outer courtyard?"

Tarrick closed his eyes.

The Emperor had found them.

Draanth.

12

*E*veryone froze in place, like a holovid on pause. Kenna had her arm outstretched, the alien weapon looking heavy and clunky in her grip, its muzzle pressed against the skull of the alien who was about to shoot Karryl. Who had yet another alien warrior pinned beneath him. All in all, it looked like a scene from a space action-adventure movie.

Cat's gaze sought the owner of the voice. At the head of a crowd, he walked down the steps like he owned the place. Which he probably did, she thought as she realized he looked like Laarn. A *lot* like Laarn. But without the scars, a little bit older, and a helluva lot bigger. What was it with these damn aliens? Why couldn't they come in normal-sized, rather than big or freaking massive? Sheesh. And Laarn thought humans were a version of the Lathar? She didn't think so. She'd never seen any human guy as big as even the smallest Lathar. Ever.

The Emperor—because everyone bowed as he passed, not to mention Tarrick's description of his uncle, it had to be the Emperor—was stripped to the waist. A light sheen of sweat that said he'd been working out covered his skin.

"Kenna. Might want to put it away," Cat said carefully, watching the Emperor as he stalked towards their little group. The guy looked scary impressive. His handsome face, so like Tarrick's and Laarn's, was set in hard lines and his body coiled with power and aggression.

She risked a glance at the other woman to find Kenna hadn't moved. Where she'd gotten the pistol, Cat had no idea. The robes they wore were great for concealment so she could have lifted from one of the warriors at any point.

"Kenna?"

The Marine shook her head, not looking away from her target even though the curiosity had to be killing her. "No can do. He puts up first, or I swear to God, I'll ventilate his skull."

At a nod from the Emperor, another warrior

peeled off from the group behind him. Like the big man himself, this one was also sweaty and stripped to the waist, but that wasn't what made the human women gawk.

He was blond.

The Lathar were almost universally dark-haired so to see one with what looked like peroxide blond short hair was startling to say the least. He moved with a dangerous grace, his heavily muscled body covered in tattoo-like designs. He wasn't young, his face lined with experience and a large scar carved a line over one cheek.

Reaching Kenna, he put a big hand on the pistol and pushed the muzzle aside. "No one will hurt the K'Vass warrior, little..." He looked down at her, then further down, taking in every aspect of her appearance. "You are one of the humans?"

Kenna refused to let go of the pistol, and a short struggle ensued, but the light-haired warrior won in the end and simply held the weapon out of reach.

"They are indeed," the Emperor strode forward, arms outstretched, "and they are welcome in my court."

He paused to cast a quick glance at the fallen warrior Karryl had pinned. With a curl of his lip that showed his disgust, he motioned for the warrior to rise. He did, slithering from Karryl's grip.

"You are a disgrace, J'aett R'Zaa. Using your warriors to end a challenge match in such a manner," he sneered. "Begone from my sight until you can conduct yourself with honor and be thankful I have not taken up the challenge on behalf of my kinsman."

The quick breath Tarrick sucked in told Cat those words were important. Leaning slightly to the side, she whispered, "I thought you said Karryl was related to you on your dad's side?"

Tarrick nodded. "He is, but by claiming kinship, Daaynal has raised our entire clan above the others, which includes Karryl."

Cat watched in carefully hidden amusement as the R'Zaa warriors scattered like fall leaves on the wind. They were obviously scared of the Emperor's wrath, and by the looks on their faces, terrified of the thought of ending up in a challenge match with him. She didn't blame them, danger and lethality oozed from the man's pores. Both he and his blond shadow were scary SOBs.

Daaynal turned to their small group and smiled as he spread his arms wide.

"Welcome to our lovely planet, Terran visitors. I

apologize for not being here to greet you, but your arrival was a little sooner than expected." He shot a small, annoyed look at Tarrick, but it was more frustrated affection than the cold fury he'd treated the R'Zaa with.

Cat breathed a small sigh of relief. She had the feeling Daaynal was not a man to piss off.

"We made excellent time, Your Imperial Majesty," Tarrick replied. "And I assumed you would want to meet the human women as soon as possible."

"Yes, indeed. Come. Come." Daaynal shepherded them up the steps and through the now open double doors. Gone was the ice-cold warrior, his eagerness to get them inside giving him the look of an enthusiastic puppy.

They followed obediently, and Cat's eyes widened at the sheer luxury that met her gaze everywhere she turned. A far cry from the stripped down practicality of their ships, the palace was like something pulled from a dream.

Cool marble, or whatever the alien equivalent was, as far as the eye could see, with high ceilings and murals on the wall to rival any of the old Terran masters. Heavy drapes of gold and silver surrounded doorways and even the guards' uniforms while the same basic design as Tarrick and his men's, had embroidered panels, sashes, and braiding. Far from appearing the poor cousins though, Cat caught the guards eyeing the battle-scarred leather with envy.

"Ahh, here we are. Come in, please!" Daaynal shoved open a set of double doors at the end of a long hallway and led them into a large room. High vaulted ceilings met tall windows open to the outside air, drapes fluttering in the pleasant breeze.

The room was occupied, around twenty people lounging on low couches, talking softly. One off to the side was playing what looked like a harp. They were mostly male, but there were a few of the oonat females Cat had seen before.

"Crap, we've walked into a *TQ* photo shoot or something," Kenna, near the back of the group exclaimed, naming a popular fashion magazine. Cat had to agree. The men were gorgeous with the lean, lithe build of models paired with the natural good looks of the Lathar.

And they left her flat. Utterly devoid of emotion. They were all pretty, but their muscles, while toned, didn't have the battle-hardened appearance of the warriors. They seemed... soft in comparison.

"Out! The lot of you...freaking useless bunch of

ingrates," Daaynal snarled, and the room cleared in seconds.

Cat watched them go, fascinated. For a culture that revered warriors, finding non-warriors was... strange. Particularly in the heart of the court.

"Who were they?" she whispered to Tarrick, but it was Daaynal who answered, turning to fix her with a direct look.

"Bloody useless. The sons of clan lords and others who owe me fealty. They're here to ensure their clan's...behavior, shall we say? Most of them have been at court since they were children."

She blinked. Now it all made sense. Warriors were dangerous, so if they hostages to ensure compliance, then Daaynal wouldn't want them trained in warfare.

"It seems..." She paused, looking for the right words, aware the Emperor watched her with interest. "I feel sorry for them. Your culture revers warriors and they aren't allowed to aspire to that."

Surprise flickered in Daaynal's eyes for a moment, then he smiled, looking at Tarrick. "Perceptive. Is this your female?"

"She is, yes. Your Majesty, may I present Sergeant Cat Moore of the Terran base, Sentinel Five."

Unsure of the protocol, Cat took the hand

Daaynal offered and attempted a small curtsy. She wobbled as she stood, catching a little smile on the Emperor's lips for a moment, but she refused to be embarrassed. How the hell should she know how to greet an emperor, especially an alien one? It wasn't like the Sentinel program ran "Alien Etiquette 101" or "Family faux pas: what to do when you meet your alien lover's royal uncle" now, was it?

"A pleasure to meet you, Sergeant Moore." Surprisingly, Daaynal didn't have any problems with deciphering human ranks and names. "Do you mind? I've never seen a human so close. Are you all this small?"

Stepping closer, he gripped her chin with strong fingers and tilted her head. Despite his size, his touch was gentle, but she did feel a little like livestock being examined. She held still, even though she wanted to squirm. Thankfully though, Daaynal's touch was impassive, not sexual, which helped her stay in place as he examined her face from all angles. Amusement filled her as she considered asking him if he wanted to check her teeth as well.

"I'm a little shorter than average for a woman," she replied, noticing he seemed just as fascinated with her hair as Tarrick had been. Perhaps it ran in the family. "But yes, we are representative of female heights. Men tend to be a little taller. Not as tall as the Lathar, though."

Daaynal nodded, his expression preoccupied.

"And they are completely compatible?" he asked Laarn, standing nearby.

"Totally."

She could feel the slight tension in Tarrick's body next to her, as though he didn't like the other male touching her. Lathar were highly possessive of their women it seemed.

"Good. Good." Daaynal nodded, his long hair dancing on his shoulders. "Nothing...strange going on down there?"

Her cheeks burned at the question as Daaynal waved at her genital region. He noticed, his gaze snapping back to her and he winked. "I don't suppose you'd like to strip so I can see for myself?"

"I'd rather not, Your Majesty."

She shook her head, her cheeks flaming. She had to be beet-red by now. The only person she planned on stripping for was Tarrick. In private though, rather than flashing her pink parts to anyone in the court who wanted to know the differences between Lathar boys and human girls.

"Perfectly understandable," he said with an easy

smile. Charm and looks...add an emperor's, what, crown...throne...and that was a lethal combination.

"Totally compatible, even with their smaller size," Tarrick said, sliding an arm around Cat's waist and pulling her against him now that Daaynal appeared to have finished his inspection.

"*Especially* with their smaller size." Karryl coughed behind them, smothering his words.

Cat kept her smile in place, ignoring the comment. She enjoyed that size difference, thank you very much, but she wasn't about to tell everyone that.

Daaynal turned to Tarrick. "Show me."

It was an order, no more, no less. Letting go of Cat, Tarrick pulled back his sleeve and removed the bracer on his wrist. The marks were there, darker than they had been. Gasps echoed around the room.

"Fuck me," Karryl muttered aloud. "Are those what I think they are?"

Laarn stepped up on Tarrick's other size as the Emperor grabbed his brother's wrist. "I would need access to the main diagnostic suites in the Healer's Hall to confirm, but my suspicion is humans are a lost branch of the Lathar. Records indicate that millennia ago, several expeditions were sent out to seed far-flung areas of the universe. Most we kept contact with, but at least three were never heard from again. My theory is humans are descendants of one of these expeditions, genetically adapted to be smaller in stature."

Daaynal shook his head, his expression one of wonder as he examined the marks on Tarrick's wrist from all angles. "Of course, whatever you need."

He lifted his head to look at Cat and once again she was struck by how much he looked like Laarn. With a better sense of humor. "Do you realize what this means?"

She shrugged, shaking her head. "All our bits fit together nicely?"

Daaynal chuckled, the tiny lines at the corner of his eyes crinkling. "No, my dear. It means you and your friends might well be the saviors of our race."

"You're getting married? Why didn't you say so?"

"I *thought* these dresses were way too fancy for a simple ball."

"Kenna...what would you know about balls? You bitched for a week straight before the last regimental ball, then got yourself thrown in the brig so you didn't have to go. Three hours of paperwork you cost me. *Three hours!* I should've just left your ass in there."

Cat stood by the window in the guest suite of the palace and let her friends' chatter fade into the background as they put the finishing touches to their outfits.

It was strange to think that a week ago she hadn't known either Jane or Kenna that well—just to nod and say hi in passing—but now she counted them among her closest friends. After all they'd been through together, she'd walk through hell and back for any of them and she knew they'd do the same for her.

They'd spent the morning being poked and prodded, then scanned and tested by Laarn in the Healer's Hall, so they had been thankful to escape to their suite for a light lunch.

When they'd arrived, they'd discovered a message from the Emperor that they were all cordially invited to escort Cat to a blessing of her union with Tarrick that afternoon. At the mention of the word 'wedding,' even the hardened Marines softened, Kenna diving into the garment bags that had been delivered with a squeal of delight.

"Ha!" Kenna threw back. "Well, look at who's all

dolled up in a dress! Looking to catch some handsome warrior's eye, are we, *Major?*"

"Screw you, brat. If anyone's after catching a warrior's eye, it's you. What about that blond hottie? Xaandril or something? He seemed mighty taken with you when we arrived."

The conversation behind her devolved into good-natured insults and name-calling between the two Marines, who from what Cat could work out, had been friends for years.

The door opened and she turned in a swish of silken skirts as Tarrick's warriors filed into the room: Karryl, Gaarn, and the quieter Talat. She hid her smile as their steps faltered when presented with the vision of loveliness her friends presented. Because the way they looked now was a far cry from the bedraggled bunch they'd been after the attack on the base.

Military uniform wasn't the most glamorous at the best of times, but throw in an alien attack, panic, and a stay in holding cells, no one would ever look their best.

Now though, with all the preening and pampering of the styling team the Emperor had arranged—comprised of vaguely insectoid looking creatures who talked, *constantly*—they'd morphed from not-quite ugly ducklings into beautiful swans.

Like Cat, they wore Latharian gowns, but where hers was the deepest sapphire, theirs were an iridescent platinum. Far from washing out their complexions, as Jane had feared the moment she'd seen them. The shifting color suited all three. Although one size, the dresses were cut cleverly and didn't overpower. Somehow they managed to give the lithe Jane curves (And boobs. Something she'd remarked on at least twice, to Cat's surprise. It seemed even uber fit Marines had hang-ups about their bodies. Go figure.) and made the fuller-figured Jess gasp in delight and scurry between mirrors checking herself out. Kenna's sole worry had been where to stash her purloined pistol. Somehow she'd managed to keep hold of it after the altercation in the courtyard.

"You look..."

For once Karryl seemed lost for words as he approached Jane. Gone was the curt, overbearing manner, and the look of frustration he seemed to have permanently around her was replaced with one of awe.

"You can say it. She looks hot. If I were into women, I'd do her," Kenna broke in, grabbing Talat's arm as Gaarn extended his for Jess. Cat noticed Jess's hopeful glance toward the door. Perhaps looking for a particular healer?

"My lady," Karryl offered his arm. "Would you do me the honor of accepting my escort to the blessing?"

"I'd be delighted." Jane smiled and inclined her head graciously. The light caught the tiny silver flowers and leaves the stylists wound through her short hair.

With all the women partnered, Karryl turned to Cat.

"Your bond-mate awaits, my lady," he said with a small bow that surprised her. He'd never bowed to her before, or called her that. Did her marriage to Tarrick confer status within Latharian society on her or something?

With an out swept arm, the big warrior signalled she should precede him.

"A lady always walks alone to meet her mate, as an indication she has chosen him of her own free will."

Huh. Interesting, and different from the human custom of giving the bride away.

"And the honor guard?" She pointed out the three warriors.

"To ensure no one interferes with your decision," he replied, then his lips quirked. "Not even your mate."

That was a new one. Cat blinked. So they'd gone from slaves and having no choice, to a situation where she seemed to have all the power. All because of a few marks on Tarrick's wrist.

"And if I decided not to go through with it?"

"Then our duty as your guard is to take you away from the hall, by force if necessary." Karryl's smile grew broader, his relish at the idea of a fight clear, but it quickly disappeared. "Although I don't want to fight Tarrick and Laarn, so please don't do that."

Cat shifted her grip on the bouquet in her hands and shook her head.

"Don't worry. I have no intention of backing out now. A gorgeous guy who actually wants to get married and have kids... do you have any idea how rare that is on Earth? Most men run a mile at the mere thought of commitment."

All three warriors glowered, their opinion of Earth men obviously not high.

"Earth men are idiots," Talat rumbled, which earned him a chuckle from Kenna, who patted his arm.

"That they are, handsome. But don't worry, there

are plenty of human women who will take one look at you and beg you to give them babies."

A distant sound, like a clarion call, stopped the conversation and Karryl urged them all toward the door. "Time to go. We do not want to be late, not with the Emperor doing this blessing."

"Good luck, Cat!" Jess called, ushered into line by Gaarn as they formed up behind Cat.

"Yeah, break a leg!" Kenna offered with a broad grin.

Jane rolled her eyes. "She's getting married, you idiot, not acting in a play!"

The doors opened and Cat stepped out. A sapphire carpet snaked in front of her so she followed it, her steps in the delicate sandals soundless on the plush surface. Guards resplendent in palace uniform lined the route to the throne room where the ceremony was to be held. They looked ahead, expressions and stances like stone, but she caught a few peeking sideways as they passed. Every now and then, one of the doors along the corridors cracked open and she spotted long-faced oonat servants peering through. Several gasped in delight when they saw her and she smiled, feeling like a real bride.

And she was.

The dress might have been sapphire rather than white or cream, but it fit her like a silken glove, the skirts swishing around her ankles before flowing into a train behind her. Her hair was gathered on top of her head in an elaborate updo, complete with a delicate tiara she'd been told came from Tarrick's family vault and she carried a bouquet in her hands. The tiny flowers looked like a cross between orchids and cherry blossoms—her two favorites. They were called Herris blossom and were apparently the symbol of the Imperial family. Only royal brides were allowed to carry them.

Huh. Her. A royal bride. Just three weeks ago she'd been convinced that the dire state of her love life meant she was destined to end up a crazy cat lady (substituting real cats with fluffy toy ones, because real cats on a station? Recipe for disaster.). Instead though, she'd hooked herself a hot, alien groom. But Karryl's words about this being her decision struck deep. Was she ready for this? Did they *need* to get married formally? Couldn't they just consider the marks on his wrist an engagement ring and date for a while?

Her heart twisted, rejecting all those ideas, and in one perfect moment of clarity, she realized why.

He'd kidnapped her, wanted her so much, he

twisted the truth to get her, then saved her from one of his biggest enemies.

He'd killed that enemy for daring to lay a hand on her...

A wash of emotion filled her chest, the warm feeling filtering out to fill the rest of her body.

She loved him.

She was head over heels, hopelessly and totally in love with her alien lord.

Tears gathered at the corners of her eyes and she blinked rapidly to clear them. Alien makeup was probably waterproof, but she didn't want to take the risk and look anything other than perfect when Tarrick saw her in her finery for the first time.

Nerves assaulted her as the carpet led to a large set of double doors. The throne room. Tarrick waited for her on the other side.

Before they reached the doors, two guards either side moved forward to open them.

Shit. This was really happening. Cat trembled, forcing to hold tightly to her flowers in case she dropped them, she shook so much. She would walk through those doors and the Emperor would bless her union with Tarrick. From what she'd been told, the marks on his wrist meant they were already married, but apparently a blessing from his

Imperialness himself conferred more status on their union. Made it *special*.

Personally, she thought their relationship was already pretty damn special. Tarrick's mating marks were the first since the last fertile Lathar female died decades ago. Ergo, special. No matter what anyone else thought.

The doors opened and a wash of noise hit her. What sounded like hundreds of people chattering, suddenly stopped to look toward the doors. Expectation filled the air, so thick she found it difficult to breathe.

They were all waiting to see her. Their first glimpse of a human woman.

"The Lady Cat Moore, of planet Earth," a loud voice announced and she walked through the door, her head held high.

Murmurs and gasps rolled through the masses either side of the aisle. Her heart tried to climb into her throat at being the center of so much attention. She focused on Tarrick's broad shoulders by the throne and started to walk. She could do this. Totally do this. Hopefully without tripping on her own skirts or otherwise making a damn fool of herself.

Her groom didn't turn, a Lathar tradition she'd been warned about, but Laarn did. His eyes widened and he leaned in to whisper something in his brother's ear.

Finally, she reached Tarrick's side and he turned his head. Emotion and reverence washed over his hard features.

"You look beautiful, Moore Cat," he whispered, reaching for her hand, his words unheard by anyone else as at that moment Daaynal stood.

13

"Warriors, welcome!" His voice carried the length of the hall. "Today we gather to celebrate a momentous event and one I didn't think we would ever see again. A true bonding."

Shock resounded through the hall in a wave of utter silence. A bonding hadn't occurred for decades. It required more than genetic compatibility, otherwise half the men in the room would have bonded to their Oonat broodmares.

Tarrick shuddered at the thought. To be bonded to a creature of such limited intelligence for the rest of his life...it didn't bear thinking about.

"Impossible!"

"How can that be?"

"She is no Lathar!"

"No marks, no bond!"

"This is an outrage!!"

Within seconds the assembled warriors had gotten over their shock and the protests came thick and fast. Tarrick closed his eyes. He recognized the loudest voice among them. Maal J'nuut was a purist, one who regularly petitioned the Emperor about the preservation of Lathar genetics. He and his clan of fanatics believed breeding with other races should be banned and the Lathar should only reproduce through cloning. As they did. It was widely known that the J'nuut eschewed the use of the Oonat, to avoid diluting their "pure" bloodline. The rumors even said Maal refused to allow his warriors Oonat women for companionship and sexual relief.

Daaynal lifted his hand and all noise in the hall ceased. "As many of you are now aware, the K'Vass recently ventured into a backwater system and discovered a previously unknown to us species. One with a pleasing appearance and many females. As soon as contact was made, the healer with the K'Vass suspected that humanity—"

"Ha! *Humanity?* What kind of name is that?"

Daaynal, interrupted, glared at the commenter

with an expression that would have frozen the fire-moons of *Dranratt*.

"As I was saying. Lord Healer Laarn K'Vass suspected humanity was genetically compatible with us."

Daaynal cast a glance down at Cat and smiled. "I am glad to say his suspicions are correct and Lord Tarrick bears evidence of this."

Stepping down from the dais, his uncle grasped Tarrick's arm and lifted it. His sleeve fell back, baring the marks on his skin. Murmurs of shock rippled through the crowds.

"A true bonding has occurred. Furthermore," Daaynal's voice turned to ice, "the entire human species is now under my protection. No clan is to invade their space, or raid any of their planets or installations. Punishment for such a transgression will be death. No challenge. No appeal, just execution. *Do I make myself clear?*"

There was no reply to the Emperor's announcement, not that Tarrick expected there to be. No one argued with such a direct proclamation, not from a man like Daaynal. Ever. He breathed a sigh of relief. With a few short sentences, Daaynal had secured the safety of the human race until proper alliances could be put into place.

"Right. Now to the matter in hand."

Daaynal stood before Cat and Tarrick and held out his hands. "Your hands please."

Without hesitation, Tarrick reached out, pleased to see Cat did the same. Her beauty always stunned him, but seeing her in the traditional robes of a Latharian bride took his breath away.

"Blood calls to blood and soul to soul," Daaynal intoned, his deep voice low and charismatic. "Soul calls to skin, woman to man, binding the halves of a whole together for all eternity. Lady Cat, do you take this warrior who bears your marks on his skin to bond-mate? To support and honor him for the rest of his life?"

She nodded, the light twinkling off the jewels in her hair. "I do."

Daaynal looked at Tarrick, his expression grave. "Lord Tarrick, do you take this woman who has called marks in your skin to bond-mate? To protect her and honor her for the rest of your life?"

"I do."

There was no other answer, he realized, standing there as Daaynal transferred their hands to one of his, binding them with a sapphire sash. Bonding them in the eyes of the ancestors.

"Then...as Emperor of the Lathar, I bless your bonding. May it bring much solace and be fruitful."

Tarrick leaned in to brush his lips over Cat's. Screw the warriors who watched, he had to touch her. She moved closer, her tiny body nestled against his and lifted her lips to his.

Before he'd registered the taste of her though, shots rang out in the hall. Energy blasts sizzled through the air, closely followed by grunts of pain and bellows of anger as warriors drew weaponry and fired back.

Tarrick whirled, shoving Cat behind him, out of danger. Fear for her pumped through his veins and in that moment he realized he would do anything, even sacrifice his own life, for her. She was his bond-mate, her life was his to protect...but it was more than that.

He loved her.

From the moment he'd laid eyes on her, he'd loved her. He hadn't realized it at the time, telling himself all sorts of lies to cover what his heart had always known. Had known from the first moment he'd heard her voice. She was the other half of his soul.

"What the hells is going on?" Daaynal demanded, his champion already at his side. Both warriors had weapons drawn, a pistol in one hand and a blade in the other.

"We will not stand for this insult!" a warrior screamed across the hall, voice raised over the sound of energy bolts. The J'nuut were gathered in a knot at the side of the room, firing wildly around them with their leader, Maal, yelling purist rants from atop a table. His face was purple, twisted with hatred as he glared across the throne room.

"*He* wishes to dilute our blood!" Maal screamed, pointing at Daaynal. "To have us consort with sub-Lathar creatures and create...abominations! Destroy what we are! He is not fit to be emperor! *Kill him! Kill them all!*"

"Well, he's a sandwich short of a picnic," Cat commented, peering around Tarrick's shoulder even as he tried to push her to safety with the other women. However, trying to keep the human women behind the relative safety of the throne was like trying to herd *viisnaas*. They'd formed themselves into a tight group, eyes bright and focused as the battle raged around them. Both Jane and Kenna somehow managed to acquire pistols, and were using the throne for cover as they fired into the J'Nuut. Each time they did, warriors fell.

"Damn good shots," Xaandril grunted, a rare

show of approval from a warrior who hated pretty much everything.

"Down, stay safe, little Cat," Tarrick ordered, shoving Cat behind the throne. When she tried to follow him, he pulled her up for a brief, hard kiss. "Please, let me protect you."

"Yeah, he's a keeper," Jess commented as the two women crouched behind the throne as the battle raged in the hall. Concern threaded through Cat's veins as she peeked out from cover. Damn Lathar and their warlike nature, not even a wedding was sacrosanct.

She picked out Tarrick and his brother, just steps from the dais, fighting off what looked like a horde of the enemy all by themselves. They moved in perfect tandem, ducking and weaving around each other. Cat gasped as Tarrick turned his back on an opponent even as the warrior lifted a blade to drive it through his chest. Without missing a beat, Laarn twisted and blocked the blow, his return swing taking the other warrior's head off at the neck. The corpse had barely hit the floor before both brothers turned and fired, dropping two more warriors about to charge them.

But it wasn't all going their way. The Emperor and his men fought on the dais, but were being picked off by snipers from the other side of the room. A warrior to their left was hit, staggering backward against the wall, then slowly slid down. His eyes were wide and lifeless before he reached the floor.

Cat scuttled over and grabbed his weaponry, ducking her head as energy bolts slammed into the wall behind her. She threw the blade to Jess and checked the charge on the pistol. Nearly full. Good. They could at least defend themselves.

"They've bottlenecked reinforcements," Xaandril yelled across at Daaynal, the two big men protecting the area at the front of the throne. "And looks like the R'Zaa have allied with the purists."

"Excellent!" Daaynal grinned as he swung the massive blade he held and lopped the arm off a warrior trying to sneak up on him. "Some real opposition then!"

Neither looked worried, in fact, both looked like they were intensely enjoying themselves. Cat shook her head. Bloody Lathar.

"Contact at twelve o'clock," Jane yelled, as

another wave of purists surged through the main doors at the end of the hall. Cat ducked out of cover, picked her target and fired. A purist fell, clutching his throat. She had to admit, as well trained as the Emperor's men were, the numbers were against them.

The situation looked dire. The end was nigh, and all that.

Then she spotted him. A single warrior, one of the R'Zaa she'd seen earlier, the ones disgraced by the Emperor, crept through the melee in the middle of the room. His attention was on Tarrick, his grip firm on the blade in his hand.

Her heart stalled. Neither Tarrick nor Laarn had seen him. A few more steps and he'd be in range. Yanking off her shoes, she darted out from behind the throne, yelling over her shoulder. "Cover me!"

They must have heard her, because energy bolts peppered the air around her as she darted through the seething mass, dropping any enemy warrior who got near her. She paid them no mind, her focus on the warrior who crept up on Tarrick, blade raised to plunge it into his unsuspecting back.

"Hey, asshole!" she called out and he whirled, eyes narrowing with malice when he spotted her. Cat's universe narrowed down to the alien pistol in her hand, hidden by her skirts, and her finger on the trigger.

She heard Tarrick's bellow, but not what he said. She was aware of the battle pausing around them as the R'Zaa bore down on her with death in his eyes.

"Say hello to your ancestors, human bitch!" he snarled, and charged.

In one smooth move, she lifted the pistol, aimed, and fired. Once, twice, three times. The first bolt hit the center of his chest, the second his throat, while the third created a starburst pattern in the middle of his forehead before the bolt shattered the back of his skull and gave him a red halo.

He staggered two more steps, then dropped like a stone at her feet. She looked down, feeling nothing at the sight of the body. He'd been about to kill her husband, on her wedding day.

Not. Happening.

"How about you say hi for me, asshole." She looked up and around. The battle had stopped, all the warriors looking at her in horrified fascination.

She smiled. "He wasn't on the guest list. Anyone else?"

The silence in the hall broke when Tarrick closed the distance between them and grabbed her upper arms, shaking her. "Cat! What the hell were you thinking? You could have been killed!"

His expression was furious, and his grip hard. She winced, trying to get free.

"In case it escaped your notice, saving your damn fool life!"

Their near shouting match was interrupted as combat bots crashed through the doors and windows, landing neatly to train weaponry on the remaining purists. There was a short fight in the corner which no one took any notice of, all eyes on the two of them in the middle of the room.

"Or would you rather I have let you be killed?" she challenged, knowing she was pushing it, but dammit, a girl had to lay down some laws. What better day to do it than on her wedding day. Besides, she hadn't promised to obey him, had she?

"Damn annoying humans." His expression shifted, his lips threatening to quirk into a smile and before she realized what he was about, he bent and threw her over his shoulder.

"Tarrick, you asshole! Put me down this instant!" she demanded, beating his broad back with her fists. Not that she thought it would make any difference.

"Problem with your bond-mate?" Daaynal inquired, his deep voice projecting amusement. Cat twisted in Tarrick's grip, trying to look at the Emperor.

"Make him put me down. Now!"

"I'm sorry, my lady, but as the lord's bond-mate, it is up to him to...errr, discipline you for any transgression of our laws."

Crap. What law had she broken now?

Tarrick bowed and she squeaked, clutching at his waist so she didn't fall. His arm was firmly over the back of her legs though, so she remained securely in place.

"Thank you, Your Majesty. If I may take my leave with my... wife?"

"Oh, *now* I'm your wife, am I? I was just damn annoying when I was saving your life!"

Daaynal answered as though she hadn't spoken. "Of course. Enjoy the rest of your bonding day."

"Thank you, we will." With that Tarrick turned and strode from the hall. Cat managed to wave at her friends, all clustered by the throne with weapons in their hands. Jess waved back just as the doors closed cutting off Cat's view of them.

"Hey! Put me down!"

Her demands were met with silence as Tarrick strode through the palace corridors. Combat bots lined them now, as well as more guards, no doubt as a result of the purist attack.

It didn't take them long to get wherever they were going, Tarrick shouldering open a door and barking an order at the bots outside.

"Now, my little mate..." He slid her down the front of his body, slowly, making sure she felt every hard muscle of his big frame. His eyes sparkled with amusement and something darker. More heated. More volatile. "How should I punish you for putting yourself in danger?"

Despite his teasing words, his hand shook when he lifted it to stroke her cheek. Stark fear eclipsed the desire in his eyes for a moment.

"Please, Cat. Never do that again. If anything were to happen to you...it would kill me. I..." He swallowed and gathered himself, looking her in the eye as serious as though he were about to go into battle.

"I love you, little Moore Cat, and without you I am nothing. I could not go on. I need you."

Tears of emotion welled in her eyes, making her vision waver.

"I'm sorry...say that again?"

He loved her? She knew he cared for her, that he couldn't get enough of her, but...loved her? She hadn't seen that coming. She didn't think the Lathar even had a word for it.

"I need you."

Stubborn man.

"No, no. Not that part. Well, I like that part, but say the bit before it again?"

"If anything were to happen to you, it would kill me?" His lips began to curve, amusement heating his alien gold gaze again. Bloody man was teasing her.

"Yes...go on."

He smiled, bent at the waist to scoop her up into his arms and carried her toward the big, circular bed in the middle of the room. "Cat Moore, lady of my heart, I love you. I've loved you since the moment I first saw you, and I will continue to love you until the end of my days. How's that?"

She sighed, reaching up to turn his face toward her as he stopped next to the bed. "Perfect. Now, Mr. Moore Cat...how about you kiss your wife?"

And he did, sealing their bonding with a kiss as he laid her on the bed. Following her down, his lips didn't leave hers. Heat enveloped them, their hands everywhere, peeling clothing away to reveal skin until they were both naked on the bed.

Cat gasped as he parted her legs with a knee, sliding between them to shelter in the cradle of her thighs. Big hands swept the hair away from her face, each touch a promise, each kiss along her throat an oath.

Reaching between them to grasp his freed cock, he rubbed the broad head between her pussy lips. She was already slick, wet for him, and the sensation of sensitive flesh sliding against sensitive flesh made them both gasp.

"Please, now..." she begged, her arms around him to hold him close. "Make me yours."

He pulled back to look her in the eye, his expression open and loving as he looked down at her.

"Mine," he murmured as he pushed forward and claimed her in one slow slide of pleasure.

"Now and forever more. Mine."

"Yours," she agreed, closing her eyes and wrapping her legs around his hips.

From her greatest fantasy and worst nightmare, she'd found the best thing any woman could wish for...

Her soul mate.

****

Ready for the next Warriors of the Lathar story?

Thank you for taking a chance on **Alien Lord's Captive**. I hope you enjoyed it!

If you did, it would be great if you could leave a **review** - even if it's just a little one. Every review makes a huge difference to an author and helps other readers find and enjoy the book as well!

I'm happy to say that the next book in the Lathar series, **Claiming her Alien Warrior** is ready and waiting for you! (Turn the page for a preview of the cover if it doesn't show!)

P.S. Check out the excerpt a bit further on for the latest book in the lathar series, **Bonded to the Alien Centurion**, which is **NOW AVAILABLE FOR PRE-ORDER!**

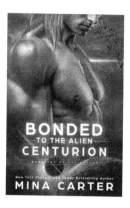

P.P.S. If you're new to me and my books, or haven't had chance to check it out yet, go take a look at my **Kyn Warriors** Series. Like the Lathar, but vampires instead!!

P.P.P.S. Sign up to my VIP mailing list and I'll shoot you a quick notification when my new books releases: **http://mina-carter.com/newsletter/**

READ AN EXCERPT FROM BONDED TO THE ALIEN CENTURION

WARRIORS OF THE LATHAR BOOK 6

"*T*ell me about these human females."

Holy *draanth*. He was in the same room as the emperor himself. Sardaan K'Vass blinked and resisted the temptation to pinch himself. Standing as he was just behind his commander, Fenriis, no one would notice if he did but that wasn't the point. He was a warrior with a headful of braids. He had a reputation to uphold. Still, he couldn't help the awe washing through him as he looked around the room. It was filled to the brim with legends.

Warriors from the other vessels crowded the room, all facing one way. Emperor Daaynal K'Saan stood there next to his sister-sons, War Commander Tarrick and Lord Healer Laarn, his grim face and scarred body a sight to behold. On the other side of the emperor was his champion, Xaandril, one arm in a sling, and, surprisingly, a human female.

Sardaan watched her from the corner of his eye. Dressed in a curious mixture of warrior's leathers and human attire, she seemed to be with Xaandril himself. That in itself was a surprise. The big, gruff champion was not known to frequent the pleasure houses and the story of how he'd lost his mate and child, and his reaction, was the stuff of legend.

Yet, he appeared protective and possessive about the little human female, glaring at any male who looked at her for too long. It was an unspoken challenge that the woman was his. If he hadn't claimed her yet, it wouldn't be long. Sardaan certainly wouldn't take him on. Even though the champion was recovering from injury, it would still be suicide.

"We have the human vice president, Madison Cole, onboard," Fenriis said, his deep voice filling the briefing room. "There seem to be some political issues. The human male, Hopkins, seems to have orders from above her, from the president himself, indicating promises she makes will not be honored."

Daaynal frowned, a deep crease between his brows. His braids, more than Sardaan had ever seen

on a warrior, brushed his shoulder as he looked at Fenriis. "You think she intends to play us for fools?"

Danaar, next to Fenriis, rumbled in the back of his throat, but the commander lifted a hand slightly to silence his second in command. Sardaan watched the interplay with interest. Danaar's feelings toward the human female were no secret. Hadn't been since the moment she'd stepped aboard their ship.

"Unsure. I do think she's being cut out of their command structure. Hopkins spouted off something about reprisals when she returns home because of her stance toward us."

There was another grumble from Danaar but he didn't speak. Like Sardaan, he knew better than to interrupt such males in conversation. But Sardaan didn't miss the tiny flicker of the emperor's gaze toward the big warrior. Shit. If Daaynal took offense...

"Her stance toward us?" the emperor continued, his attention once again on Fenriis. "A good one, I take it?"

Fenriis nodded. "Seems level-headed and open to both negotiation and the possibility of integration of our two species."

"One species," the Lord Healer interrupted.

"Humans are a subspecies of Lathar. They literally are us. But smaller."

"And we still have women," the woman at Xaandril's side interrupted, something that made more than a few males around the room frown. But neither the emperor nor the lord healer seemed annoyed, instead nodding in agreement as the woman spoke.

"Madison Cole is a good woman," she continued. "Fair and level with good policies. She's always fought for the people, even against overwhelming odds, and it doesn't surprise me that she's being reasonable about human-Lathar negotiations. *Nor* does it surprise me," she stressed quickly, "that the asshats in Terra-command are moving against her. They've been trying to discredit her for years. She's good people."

Sardaan watched her openly now, along with most of the room. Daaynal smiled. "Gentlemen, please let me introduce Kenna Reynolds, one of our delightful Terran guests. She has been most gracious in aiding our understanding of her people."

Sardaan easily decoded the emperor's words. The woman had to be one of the women taken from the first Terran base the Lathar had discovered. Stories had been going around about them since

their discovery. They were all supposed to be military women. Now, having seen her and others on the human ship just off their port bow, he finally understood what that meant.

Kenna lifted her chin, looking around the room with a slight smile on her lips as she nodded in acknowledgment. "Gentlemen."

"So... you think dealing with the vice president will get us nowhere?" the emperor demanded of the human female, who shrugged.

"Without knowing more about the situation and speaking to her, I can't say that. I've been out of the loop for a while."

She flashed a grin at Xaandril, and Sardaan was surprised to see the slight softening of his features as he looked at the tiny female. Yeah, the champion had it bad. Why hadn't he claimed her yet? She was right there, and much smaller than the champion. There was no way she'd be able to win in a challenge fight.

"Who else are we dealing with?" Daaynal transferred his attention back to Fenriis. To his credit, the war commander didn't even flinch in the face of the emperor's harsh manner, but Sardaan hadn't expected anything else. They were all K'Vass, the best warrior clan out there.

"The human ship *TSS Defiant* originally arrived commanded by a General Hopkins, but after his attempted attack on us, command transferred to a Major General Black. Female. I can't tell how old she is, I..." Fenriis shrugged a little. "My exposure to females has been limited. If I were to guess, I would say she's a warrior in her prime."

The image of the beautiful Terran woman formed instantly in Sardaan's mind when Fenriis mentioned her name, and he kept his expression level only with hard-fought control. As communications officer, he'd been the first to speak to her and had been instantly captivated. She was tiny and beautiful... her direct gaze affected him on levels he'd never experienced before, and he instantly wanted more. He'd kill to get her into a challenge circle and claim her.

"Wait..." Kenna butted in, her expression rapt. "Did you say Major General *Black*?"

Fenriis nodded, the males around the table looking at the human female. She certainly had all of Sardaan's attention. Any information he could glean on Black was good. If he ever managed to meet her, he wanted as much intel as possible to further his interests.

"You know this name?" Daaynal asked.

Kenna whistled, and nodded. "Oh yeah... I know Black. *Everyone* in the service knows Black."

"Explain." The emperor's demand was brusque and would have made a lesser warrior quake in their boots but Kenna's lips merely quirked.

"Black is a legend in her own lifetime. Like a seriously scary lady. Been in just about every conflict...like ever. Totally badass."

His human female was a warrior like him.

Sardaan couldn't help the small grin that passed over his lips. *Badass*. Even he could work out the human word was a good one. Black would make a worthy mate indeed... once he got near enough to claim her. He cast a quick glance at the males around the table. Half looked as interested in information on Black as he was. *Draanth,* he'd probably have to fight for the chance to claim her.

He gritted his teeth as determination filled him. He would do whatever he had to. She was *his*. It would be good to have a mate, someone to share his life with. She would soon adapt to life on board a Latharian vessel.

"Good. Then we need her on-side, preferably mated to one of our warriors," Daaynal announced, looking at Fenriis.

For a moment Sardaan's heart almost stopped in

his chest, but then he remembered that Fenriis already had a mate, the lovely Lady Amanda. "Commander, you are the only one of us who has actually spoken to the female in question at length. Opinion?"

"She's a capable warrior and in my opinion, nobody's fool. She will not be easily manipulated. However, during the conversation I had with her earlier, she did betray interest, a very small interest, in one of our warriors."

Sardaan blinked, replaying the conversation in his mind as he tried to figure out who Fenriis was talking about—and, more importantly, who he'd have to kill to get a shot at the female he wanted—but came up blank.

There had been interference on the line during the communication, so he'd had to pay attention to his systems to keep it cleaned up. He'd taken his attention off the screen a couple of times.

"Who?" the emperor demanded.

Fenriis turned to the side slightly, leaving Sardaan himself in the spotlight. He half turned before he realized there was no one behind him.

"Me?" His voice betrayed his surprise, and then pleasure flooded his system. Black had shown

interest in *him*? Perhaps this would be easier than he'd thought.

"Yes, you. Your Highness, this is Sardaan K'Vass, a kinsman of mine." Fenriis gave a small smile as he urged Sardaan to step forward. "There was a slight flicker of her gaze toward him during our communication and in a woman like that..."

Sardaan nodded, stunned at both the fact Fenriis had named him as kinsman and the revelation of Black's interest. Sure, he *was* distantly related to the war commander—they shared a cousin—but to have the male confirm their link in front of the emperor, no less. It was a step up for sure. Then to realize the woman he'd been so affected by had apparently noticed him as well... Black had been so controlled during all the communications that such a lapse was telling.

"Excellent!" The emperor beamed. "Sardaan K'Vass, you will be the major general's escort for this evening. I want you to stick to her like *pelaranss*. Ply her with drink and get into her bed. If you can get her to accept your claim over her, even better. Do not fail us on this. Understand?"

"Yes, sire," he said with a bow. This time he couldn't stop the slow grin that spread over his face.

Seduce the woman of his dreams with the emperor's blessing? He was *all* over that.

"I won't let you down. She'll be mine before sunrise."

PREORDER YOUR COPY NOW!

ALSO BY MINA CARTER

Claiming her Alien Warrior

In a race against the clock, she must betray his trust to achieve her mission... But fooling a Latharian warrior comes with a price.

A guest of the Lathar, Jane Allen hasn't forgotten what she is: a hard as nails marine major. Tasked with finding a way to beat the technologically advanced, biologically superior warrior race, she needs to find answers for her superiors... before they arm the nukes and give the Lathar an excuse for war. Because the little green men aren't so little. Or green... they're large, ripped, scarily-attractive alpha male warriors hot enough to make any red-blooded woman weak at the knees. Especially one particular warrior with black hair and a sexy growl she can't resist...

She's his... she just doesn't know it yet.

Karryl K'Vass has wanted the little human warrioress, Jane, from the moment he saw her. But she's a tricky one, evading his claim even though he knows she desires him. His campaign for her heart is stalled when duty calls him away; a mission into a dangerous part of space to gather intelligence on the Empire's enemies. A beautiful

stowaway is the last thing he needs, even if she does make his body burn. He'll finish his mission and get her back to the safety of Lathar Prime...

But no plan survives contact with the enemy. Reptilian mercenaries, a crash landing, and a case of amnesia later and they land in the clutches of their enemies who think it would be better if Karryl took a long walk out of a short airlock...

GET YOUR COPY NOW!

http://mina-carter.com/books/claiming-her-alien-warrior/

Pregnant by the Alien Healer

She's pregnant without nookie. Someone slap her ass and call her Mary...

A 'guest' of the Lathar, Jess has become used to being at court, especially as it allows her to be close to a certain tall, handsome healer. But Laarn might as well not know she exists, far more interested in his tests and her genetic code than her as a woman... maybe. A hot encounter after a combat trial prove that Laarn HAS noticed her, more than noticed her. But before they can act on the attraction between them, Laarn is called away to the battlefield leaving Jess all alone at court.

Not wanting to both any of the other healers when she feels unwell, Jess gets treatment from the automated systems in Laarn's lab, only to get worse days later. She's pregnant, without a sniff of between the sheets action and worse, there's a bunch of fanatics loose in the palace trying to kill her and her baby...

He aches to claim her, but saving his people must come first. To do that, he can't waste time with a female...

Lord Healer for the Lathar, Laarn must find a way to save his people from the plague that claimed all their women a generation ago. Now it speeding up and if he doesn't do something, the Lathar will be gone in a generation. Salvation arrives in the form of humanity, descendants of a lost Lathar colony, who might just hold the key to reversing the damage to the Lathar genetic code.

His scars mark his rank, but will they also lose him the woman he loves?

Laarn never thought anything of his scars before. In his culture they mark his rank as the best healer in the empire, but he starts to cover them when Jessica, the delicate little human female who holds his interest, won't look at them. He wants her, but his duty lies elsewhere until everything changes...

Between a pregnancy, mating marks and a fanatic out to kill the woman he loves, can Laarn remain detached enough to do his duty... or will he give into emotion and save his heart?

GET YOUR COPY NOW!

http://mina-carter.com/books/pregnant-by-the-alien-healer/

ABOUT THE AUTHOR

Mina Carter is a *New York Times & USA Today* bestselling author of romance in many genres. She lives in the UK with her husband, daughter and a bossy cat.

WANT THE LATEST NEWS AND CONTESTS? SIGN UP TO MINA'S NEWSLETTER!
http://mina-carter.com/newsletter/books/

Connect with Mina online at:
mina-carter.com

facebook.com/minacarterauthor

twitter.com/minacarter

instagram.com/minacarter77

amazon.com/Mina-Carter

bookbub.com/authors/mina-carter